MASQUE

Every writer has a monster in them. Some are very beautiful. This novel is for all of them.

MASQUE

BETHANY W POPE

SEREN

Seren is the book imprint of
Poetry Wales Press Ltd
57 Nolton Street, Bridgend, Wales, CF31 3AE
www.serenbooks.com
Facebook: facebook.com/SerenBooks
Twitter: @SerenBooks

The right of Bethany W. Pope to be identified as
the author of this work has been asserted in accordance
with the Copyright, Designs and Patents Act, 1988.

ISBNs
Pback – 978-1-78172-324-1
Ebook – 978-1-78172-325-8
Kindle – 978-1-78172-326-5

A CIP record for this title is available from the British Library.

The publisher acknowledges the financial assistance of the Welsh Books
Council.

Cover Design: 'At the Masquerade' by Charles Hermans, photo of Palais
Garnier by Charlotte Chen, Flickr: Labmove /CC BY-SA 2.0, back cover
image 'Curtain' by Shelah, Flickr: Gosheshe /CC BY 2.0.

Printed by Latimer Trend & Company Ltd, Plymouth.

CHRISTINE

1.

I have everything I ever thought I wanted: a room of my own made for opera, a voice to fill it, a brazier to warm the air and my throat, and a door that locks – the outside painted with a version of my name enclosed inside a star. The mirror is beautiful but that's all, a rococo frame, gilt around a smooth surface; like so many operas.

I live for the high notes; I serve the occasional glorious aria that redeems a base plot. My voice brings life to the story; my face makes the room seem populated. There are three faces in the mirror and I am looking at them. I am alone and not alone.

The features are a little blurred; they don't look like they belong to me. The flaws in the right and left wings (beneath the fat and leering putti that glower from the frame) make the sides seem warped. The glass bulges out so that my cheeks might belong to a skull, scraped to bone. Only the front view is clear, recognisable, a dark-eyed, dark-haired woman who must, every night, resemble a girl. Not just any girl but the black-eyed thing I was twenty years ago. It's funny how much a change in angle, in perspective, warps something that should be so simple. It's funny how stasis can look so beautiful, so calm at a distance and be so monstrous up close.

The girl knocks. I cannot for the life of me remember her name. Some ballerina rat doing double duty as dresser, as I did once. I rise to admit her. The pink silk frock that Fiordiligi, the Lady from Ferrara, wears in *Così fan tutte* rustles at the elbows. Locks never work for me but it comforts me to use them. I let her in. A thin-faced blonde, her dancing shoes already strapped, the satin safe behind chamois savers designed to keep the delicate soles from scuffing. As if anything could save our souls. She looks like poor Little Meg, a girl I knew once and haven't thought of in years. No. That's a lie. I see her every day. She takes her turn in the mirror, with all the others I've loved.

This girl, whoever she is, twitches her nose at me. She might be smelling the blood in my neck – or some other, less mentionable, middle-aged woe.

'La Changy?' Her voice is rough, trained she might make a mezzo. As it is, she sounds like a whore with a cough.

'Yes?' I am spared impropriety; it would be unfitting if I knew her name. Divas should never nurse rats, should never take the ugly (the ordinary) to their breasts.

'The new manager, Mr Andre, send his regards. And some new perfume.'

The name makes me start, but there are only a few families wealthy enough to found operas in Paris. The bottle is huge, blown glass, indigo flowers. It would be unpolitic not to wear it. He would notice if my throat smelled only of my artistic sweat.

I nod to the rat, the girl. I have just remembered her name. 'Apply it, Juliette. A drop.'

Her smile is hideous. Her teeth are yellow and few. She will be a dancer until she drops. Those incisors of hers might save her from syphilis. If so they only seem like ugliness. They have softened me to her. I bend down, almost bowing. I can feel her meaty, spoiled breath on my skin, overpowering the scent of opal fruit and ylang ylang flowers. The glass applicator is cold and wet. It feels like she is tasting my jugular, waiting for me to start feeding her.

Tonight I will leave her a good tip.

2.

I was a lucky rat. The countess who buried my father only *looked* like an icicle. Her clear skin and white hair concealed a good heart. I do not say a 'warm' heart. Everyone alive has one of those lying, fluttering monsters. She was a good mistress, unchristian in her desires but Christian in her dispersal of them. She did not keep me as a lover, as wealthy people (even women) could do then, but she held me as her ward. I had a bedroom in her house just beyond the servants' quarters. I didn't have to lodge at the opera house and pay for the privilege of studying there with the sweat of my body. I didn't have to buy my food by wrapping my thighs around some rich gentleman's waist. Her kindness saved me from disease, and splinters.

Of course I was lonely. I had status among the other dancers because of her money and my sweet smell, but they hardly spoke to me if they could avoid it. After all, what subjects did we share? I was not hungry. Aside from that, I worked as a chorister.

My voice, at first, was less pure than it had been when I still sang for my father, but enough quality remained for me to sing small roles; a second sister, a Maying maid. They actually paid me for that, on a sliding scale, depending on the take in the production. Of course the regular singers had little to do with me, except for the sessions I spent learning from the Music Master (the countess paid for those). It would have been improper for a cast member whose art was 'pure' to speak with a singer who also worked as a dancer.

Little Meg was an exception. Her face was thin, and hollow (she sold her teeth to buy her mother free from jail) but she was a beautiful dancer. She was the highest-paid member of the company who wasn't a musician or a singer, even surpassing the salary of La Sorelli – the beautiful girl who enjoyed the affection of the Opera House owner. Little Meg had been educated a bit before her father left, she'd learned to read, and she paid for her lessons by selling painters the privilege of placing her image on canvas.

She was a wonderful conversationalist. I never met a girl with more fondness for books. Once I'd worked around her lisp we had some beautiful talks. I brought her story books after I was finished with them. It was good to feel needed and it reminded me of the time I spent with Father before he died.

She would come in post-production, help free me from whatever lousy wig they'd put me in, and check behind my ears for nits. Then I'd help her clean the wounds on her feet, scrape the scabbing blood from the satin shoes she was still paying the company for and afterwards we would crouch together by the fire and eat some bread, some good camembert (she softened the crusts of her rolls in a mug of warm wine) and we would burn the energy of performance out in conversation. There were never words enough, or time. I still miss her, even now, after everything. I still listen for the sound of her breathing in the dark.

3.

The Opera House was built like a skull beneath the skin, ugly bones beneath some beautiful flesh. The part the public saw was like my mirror, all gilt wood and plush. Behind the scenes the wood was rougher, with the mechanics of scenery flitting (and occasionally grinding) like thoughts. The flies were filled with ragged men who stank and cursed as they drew the ropes. The dressing rooms reeked with the stench of feet and foul water from the pots, the few sticks of furniture were feathered with piles of sodden costumes waiting to be cleaned – the fresh ones were delivered weekly from the cleaners – and since we used them in common (unless we had a named role) the fabric was always slick and clammy with sweat that was only occasionally our own.

Only the big stars, La Carlotta, Senior Piangi, Monsieur Jacques, earned their own rich rooms. The one I have now is nicer than theirs ever were – plumbing has improved since then, and the only bottom to warm my sofa is my own – but back then they were heaven beside what we knew. Oh, how I envied La Carlotta's silken walls! Now I know that the brilliant colour of the yellow wallpaper had been set with arsenic, but I only saw the surface then, and it was as glorious as her own pampered flesh. It is amazing that it did not kill her, or her appetite. Every night after she performed she would sit down to a supper large enough to feed a small family. Until she'd had it, she was unfit to meet the public. No matter how adoring they were, how many gifts they gave her, she would snarl at them if she hadn't had her bread and meat.

La Carlotta was as famous for her bosom as for her silk-sweet larynx. When she hit those high notes in, say, the aria that Elisabeth sings in act five of *Don Carlos*, the heaving was magnificent, just this side of decency. She padded them, boosted her bosoms with rolled cotton bolsters to preserve their fine shape. I know that now (and I've mastered that trick myself) but the effect from the stage was not to be missed.

I saw those fatty flesh-waves when it was my job to turn her out before a show and I had to wedge her into stays made for a smaller-figured woman. How she sang like that, and looked so delicate, I will never know. Off stage she walked with a heavy thump, the flesh of her thighs and buttocks wobbling on her narrow ankles. Say what you will, the woman had style and style is sister to art, and she practised intensely for five hours a day, eating like the workhorse she was between the rehearsal and the show.

We all took turns acting as her dresser. It was good work. The diva screamed a lot when things weren't perfect, but after she had eaten something she often repented and would leave a good tip. Of course, once the trouble began she rarely tipped me.

She would sit terribly still as I freed her coarse black hair from the pins that bound to her braids those yellow silk strands that some poor woman had sold to the wigmaker, her face pale and moist as fresh dough. It was almost as though she feared I would bite her. It took me years to work out why. She was right to be afraid. She knew what time was; I had no knowledge of it.

ERIK

1.

My father was a master mason. I never met the man but I spent the first decade of my life inside the house he built and so I feel I know him. The lathes of the attic communicated with me as much through their shape (he was exacting when he laid out the angles of the eaves) as did the notations he left in pencil on the undersides of the unfinished, unpainted struts which supported the ceiling. I inherited the crabbed handwriting he used to mark out his measurements, though I am far more articulate than he ever was in artistry, architecture, or print.

Although he was skilled with the trowel and could lay travertine so tightly that its texture was more like marble than limestone, he was more renowned for the beauty of his person that the skill of his hands. He won my mother with his looks and he left her a sad ghost of the gay girl he married, haunting the house that he built on Rue Rouge.

I learned about him through the letters he left to my mother, retained by her in memory of their apparently passionate courtship. They were bound by a blue ribbon, an appropriate memento of an innocent girl. One envelope contained a bright lock of hair that must have been his, since mother's was as dark as a sewer rat's. The letters were naïve, almost innocently crude. They were full of phrases about the things that he wished that he could do to her body and peppered with prayers for many years of marital bliss. They were written in the kind of cheap ink that an uneducated man would favour. He did not expect them to last, or be held on to. The sepia was grainy and badly mixed, this combined with his handwriting in such a way that it seemed as though his words were written out by a sexually precocious child with a fondness for experimenting with matchsticks. As I said, my handwriting is no better, but at least the ink I use is superior.

I always thought that writing was a bit like the telepathy those spiritualists in the paper are always talking about. It makes sense, if you think about it; one mind communicates to another through a series of black blotches which transmit thoughts directly into another's brain. You, reading this, whoever you are, can hear my voice (a sweet, trained tenor) without ever having to worry about viewing the flesh that produces it. This is lucky for you: all my gifts are internal.

In any case, my current habitations remind me of my childhood home. These damp vaults are rather like the basement where my mother moved my crib once the neighbours complained that my cries disrupted their business. The house my father built was tall and narrow, the walls of dark grey granite, polished to the high shine of gravestones. He meant his home to be a living monument to his skill and a permanent advertisement for his services.

The roof was tiled with slabs of greenish slate, and the windows were small and imperfectly glassed. When I was older, I replaced them as a gift for my mother. I spent a whole afternoon removing the warped and watery panes, replacing them with sheets I'd poured myself. I learned the art of glazing, sneaking every night to the factory down the street. When the time came that I had spent enough hours watching the midnight production shift pouring the sheets of reddish molten sand into the mould, I tried my hand at it myself. I waited until the Michaelmas holiday and stole the machinery (I provided my own materials, lugging bags of silicone that I'd found in the cellars among the unopened bottles of wine and the skeletons of rodents). I love the look of glass as it is being poured. It is honest, then, about itself. Cooled, it only seems a solid. It never fully hardens. Over centuries, window glass will melt.

There is no such thing as stasis.

In any case, my mother loved the finished product; windows that let the light in without warping what she saw on the street. She was so thrilled she squeezed my upper arm through the thick fabric of my jacket. I swear she almost hugged me. In any case, for once she did not shudder at my smell or flinch away from the feel of my corpselike body.

The houses on either side of ours were dedicated, in their own way, to music. Dancing girls and cabaret, absinthe and cheap champagne that the likes of those poets who styled themselves 'Romantic' drank themselves to death in. My widowed mother hired men to refurbish the attic into a series of rooms that she furnished with sticks she'd bought from brothels, closed in raids by the province governor the previous summer. She did not sleep on them and rarely bothered to change the sheets, so she didn't have to worry about bedbugs. She made a good living, I must say, giving the drunks who seethed from her neighbours in the early morning a bed off of the streets.

For my fifth birthday she made me my first (and for a long time only) birthday present; a mask cut from a length of chamois that she bought from a glover. It was more like a loose sack with holes cut for eyes than a proper garments but it did its job well. The sight of me ceased bothering her. As I grew older, she let me come up more frequently – although once she had a steady stream of lodgers I never had the run of the attic again – my father's writing was long since buried behind plaster. I wore the mask without complaint – it was far from uncomfortable and it had a nice smell, as did the sachets of mint and violet that she sewed into my clothing. If she almost never touched me, she did love me as best as she was able, being young and easily frightened.

After a few years of proving my capacity with panes of glass and basic home repairs, she hired a blind tutor to teach me letters, music, mathematics. He would come and sit for hours in my basement room, complaining of the effect of the chill on his bones and making me memorise many disparate packets of learning. When I surpassed his ability to teach, as I soon did, I had many books close at hand and I turned to them to expand my knowledge. I read everything from Archimedes to fairy stories. As I recall, I had a special affection for *La Belle et la Bête*. My mother bought me as many books as she could afford through mail-order – often secondhand. She resold them after I had squeezed them of their nutrients, though I demanded permission to keep the fairy tales. They were a balm to me, with their stories of transformation. They provided me with a sharp and dangerous hope.

I could read as much as I liked, as long as I remained hidden. It would not have done for me to frighten the lodgers. I was happy, very happy, while I had enough books and candles. I do not believe that anyone but mother and the old tutor knew that I was still alive. The neighbours probably believed that I died in infancy. It certainly would have been safer for Mother to spread that rumour, given the prevalence of local superstition and a widespread belief in 'changelings'.

When I turned thirteen, she sent me to school.

2.

I lived for five years with the Sisters of the Daughters of Charity of Saint Vincent de Paul. They were known locally as the 'Grey Sisters' because of their granite-coloured habits and starched white veils that rose into peaked horns from the sides of their heads. These nuns ran a school for the troubled gifted (a category that fitted me like a glove) where they provided care for the physically weak and specialised learning for the intellectually advanced. The school was founded in 1640 near the centre of the city but disbanded after the failed revolution – the nuns hid while the trampled and impoverished citizens that they'd once fed hosted gallows-staged puppet shows with the decapitated corpses of their oppressors.

One extremely elderly lady was a novice at the time when Reason reined from her bloody throne. She sat crouched in her chair (carved from the unbroken trunk of a thorn tree) and muttered horrors to us while her rheumy green eyes blazed from the loose folds of her face.

'You think that you've known terror, child?' Sister Mercy leaned in close to me, her nose brushing the kid mask above the place my nose was not.

I nodded at her, silent. I was conscious of the effect that my voice had on women. The mixture of attraction and repulsion that I provoked when I spoke would have been alarming to see in a nun – especially a virgin lady who had lived so long as to be nearly able to match me in ugliness.

She laughed, a sound like a frog caught in a sausage-grinder. A connoisseur of sound even then, I stored it away for future reference, to practise at my leisure. I sat on my heels, listening in the ashes of the stove.

'Well, child, you haven't seen anything until you've seen the rotting corpse of a sixteen-year-old virgin hung from ropes hooked into her thighs, above the knees, her wrists, and the ragged stump of her neck so that she can be made to act out a play by that old rascal Robespierre. I saw this many times, starring different ladies of course. The puppets could hardly be made to last beyond a few performances. The stench would get too bad, the muscles would liquefy so that they slid from their hooks like a soft-boiled egg strung on a wire. They'd smell worse than you do, you little living corpse.'

She cackled again, scratching her scabby bald head beneath her veil.

'I liked looking at it. Sometimes they'd be wearing their fine clothes; sleeves to the elbow, trailing lace, with those high white wigs wedged onto their neck-stumps. Sometimes they'd be naked as a sparrow and sitting close to the stage (I survived by dressing up in boys' clothes, a crime then and now). I could see straight through the hair to their never-you-mind-it. Hehehe, it was lovely. Not that you'll ever get to see one, you poor little freak. Just you wait, you'll get your architect's training, all the learning you'll want, and then my younger sisters will call in the Cardinal. He'll examine you. You'll pass, no doubt about it. And then you'll be an architect priest in the service of Blessed Pope Pius IX. The good news, my lad, is that when that happens no one will care what you look like. You'll give service to

God, and that'll be more than enough for anyone.'

Eventually the old nun would tire of tormenting me with stories and fall asleep, her hairy chin pinning her breast like the church-wall illustrations of the pelican which fed its children with the blood of its heart.

I got along with the elderly, with Sister Mercy and her ilk. The other children were another matter. The boys and girls were housed in different schools. I had lived to eighteen without ever meeting a female that was not either a relative or beyond the borders of menopause. As for the boys, none of them would consent to share a room with me, not that I blamed them.

Not one of them had ever seen my face, but my limbs, my mask, were enough to frighten these 'troubled angels'. Some of them were soft in the head and very easily frightened. Others were sharper, but they had been so steeped in superstition, so inculcated with fear, that they would not dare to approach the child they called Le Mort Viva. I did not have to live in the basement here, among the dust and the skeletons of rats, but neither was I friends with any other pupils. I had my own room, far from the others, in a high tower, girded close round with ivy. It gave me plenty of space to continue my experiments with mirrors, magic, music and glass.

The old nun was half-right, in the end. I was very well educated. The Prioress hired a specialist from the university to give me private lessons. He was the only adult male voice I ever heard behind those tall limestone walls, the only baritone among the vine-drenched walls. Most of the boys returned to their families soon after puberty, called home to resume the work of their dead fathers. Only I lingered. His laughter echoed even in rooms muffled by religious tapestry.

We sat in the library, surrounded by books bound in good leather, donated by the local wealthy in an effort to purchase entry into heaven. I was tall for my age, almost six foot, and stronger than I looked despite the skeletal appearance of my limbs. I once bent a pewter spoon in half just to see if I could. I did it easily, although the skin of my hands tore like the rind of a cheese and left greyish tatters on the handle. Sitting in the comfortable Chippendale chair (another donation from the wealthy to the poor) I could almost have passed for a man – or the remnants of one. A corpse with a face behind a shroud of goat skin.

The master, Mr Garnier, was short and nearly as bald as I am. He had a tidy, fat stomach (its roundness emphasised by a thick gold watch chain) and a white goatee beneath a cleanly shaven lip. He stood above the desk, quizzing me, 'And what have you learned about Mr Claude Nicolas Ledoux and his Barriere des Bonshommes?'

This was almost too easy, 'They are facades designed to imitate the perfection of the ancient Greeks – a popular current style.'

His jolly face clouded, 'And nothing at all like these things you are drawing. Look at this filth! Naked pagan gods, goddesses with bared breasts, all these carved plants that are to be dipped in gold. The church will never sponsor it. You are a gifted lad, Erik, but like every artist you must know your audience. What exactly is this supposed to be?'

'An opera house.' I looked at my long fingers, still scabbed from bending the spoon. The raw flesh dyed with ink. Why, I wondered, could I draw and sketch so easily and yet have so much difficulty with calligraphy?

My master was silent. He turned from my chair, towards the window. I was used to open windows, even in the cold.

It was a rule, among the sisters, to maintain good ventilation when I was around.

'You do not wish to pursue a career in the church?'

'Not particularly. God prefers perfection, as far as I can tell. I can only give that in architecture.'

Monsieur Garnier smoothed the designs I'd drawn. His forehead wrinkled. Smoothed. He said, 'Let me take these away for a few days. It will be a delicate manoeuvre getting you out of the door and into the world, but I may have something for you yet.'

As it turned out, I did not have very long to wait.

3.

'It's nothing like reading about it in books, is it my lad?' Master Garnier clapped his fat hand on the blade of my shoulder. His face crumpled instantly with rank regret at the feel of my flesh through five layers of fine fabric. He was always forgetting what it was like to touch me. Once a day, at least, he would clap or cuff me when I had pleased him with my work, exactly the way the more masculine nuns would playfully strike the boys they liked best.

I cannot say how much I despised his regret. I cannot tell how much I loved my master for forgetting, so constantly, his repulsion.

'No,' I said, leaning out across the parapet to watch as my designs blossomed in the desert, a fabulous fortress in praise of the flesh. 'The books say nothing of the joy of this, of the pleasure that comes with forming something wonderful on paper and watching it grow to life in stone. They say nothing of the fear that some uneducated fool will foul my structure because he cannot see the logic or the cost. It is rather like that time that I composed a fugue for Sister Theresa. It was perfect in my mind, and my hands were perfect on the organ, but those idiot children marred five notes out of ten, singing flat, so that the ghost of my intentions emerged without the full force of the spirit I used to bring them into the world. I am more afraid of almost succeeding than I am of failure.

We were silent for a moment, a blast from the desert carried rough sand and the faint scent of roses from the harem. I hated the sand. It caught in the folds of the garments I wore and grazed my paper-thin cheeks, abrasions which opened into bright, weeping sores. In spite of what I knew about myself, I feared scarring. No one ever wishes to be worse than they must be.

'Why are these emotions never written down, Master?' I turned to meet his gaze, as much of it as I could considering our adoption of the local Muslim custom. His eyes were shadowed by a small, round cap pressed into a square of fabric in red check. In our new white robes and with our covered faces it was almost possible to ignore my mask. For the first time in my life I felt almost ordinary, almost passable. I loved the feeling, and loathed it.

His round, wrinkled face crumpled into a smile at that question.

'Erik, you are young after all, in spite of your work. There is a paradox in every vein of art I've found, that makes it nearly impossible for a genius to grow in reputation, in their own lifetime, at least, without pretending to ordinary people that anyone could make the miracles they do.' His hand went out for my shoulder again. This time he forced it to remain there, though his fingers trembled. In my soul, I thanked him for the effort.

'Politics, my boy. Some of the greatest enemies to the arts are in the arts themselves. They are the gatekeepers you must bow to in order to progress and make your great work in spite of them, and right before their faces.'

I could feel his fingers thrumming, his very tendons desiring flight. He forced our connection, continuing, 'The greater the genius, the deeper the bow they expect. My boy, they will try to make you grovel.'

I patted his hand, thanking him, disgusting him, releasing him at once. Oh what, I thought, would they think of me in the harem? I rather expected that inside those smooth pink-marble walls it would be very like the nunnery; with perhaps fewer garments. The air was perfumed, but a room full of women must be as bad, in this heat, as a room full of cats. I must say that Persia gave me beautiful dreams.

'I have grovelled enough and been hidden enough, for one lifetime. It is dishonest to bow before the middling. A mercy to them, perhaps, like my mask, but a lie even so. I won't do it.'

'Well, my boy, no one is asking you to, yet.' His smile was strained and his hands kept wiping at the hem of his robe. He thought I didn't notice. 'Come. Let's get down there and do what we are paid for. Make sure that horrid foreman is not stealing more cement.'

'Ug, how I loathe him. I would happily kill him for cutting corners on that fountain. And those looks he gives me!' I grinned, nearly lipless, luckily invisible, 'And they say that I have got an evil face.'

We took the winding stair down to the street. I approved of the gilt wood and lush carvings of stylised, almost feminine animals lining the banister. My fingers traced the outlines of lionesses, graceful, dashing gazelles.

Raoul

1.

I'm not used to failure yet, or to the complexity of fulfilment and desire. I never knew that I could get something I thought I wanted, be satisfied with it for a while, and then discover that the chocolate was bitter beneath the bright foil. Perhaps my brother should have denied me more often; perhaps he should have allowed the nurse who played the role of my mother sometimes, to inhabit that state more fully, to allow both 'Yes' and 'No'.

It has only just occurred to me that all three of us grew up with one dead parent. We've all lived with ghosts. My father survived, just barely, until I was sixteen. I was a late arrival; the product of a third wife, a pretty young thing purchased from her parents to warm the bed of a man sixty years her senior. I was the unexpected pregnancy which killed her. She wasn't bought for breeding. Her narrow pelvis could not spread. It is difficult to know that your first act on earth slaughtered your mother.

Now we all are orphans.

Still, it was a happy childhood. I lived with my nurse on the Brittany coast while my brother lorded it over Paris, preserving our fortune by investing in shipping and pretending to philanthropy by spreading coppers to the arts. I knew, even then, that he had a mistress, a dancer. Well, he was forty years old and unmarried. He needed distraction.

I was well educated in the subjects I loved: art, music and seafaring. Maths and history fell by the wayside. I rarely made it all the way through novels. I have since learned that because authors put what they know in their books, and since only so many things can happen to us (humanity is limited), a novel could have told me the story I would live before it happened. I would have known the structure of the terror anyway, known how to act to save her. I might have discovered what she was. At least, if I'd still failed, I wouldn't have had to meet it as though I'd invented the emotions I suffered.

I have slogged my way through many stories since; I have the time after all. I keep seeing her, my perfect image of her, dressed in the robes of Persephone, lodged in the underworld, her lips bleeding pomegranate seeds which glisten in the gloaming dark.

I remember the first time I saw her. We were almost still children, exactly the same age: fourteen and a day. She was a wild, ragged thing, swathed in white silk that had been quite fine the week before when her patron, the Countess, purchased it in Paris. Heaven only knows how she soiled it so quickly. It would be very like Christine to drench herself in delicate silk and then go rolling down the sand dunes to play in the waves.

Her father, the genius, was standing beside the Countess (she shaded him with her pink lace parasol – I think she was a little in love with him) playing gypsy reels on his lovely honey-coloured violin. It sang nearly as sweetly as Christine did, dancing there, dark as Salomé, twirling her red brocade scarf like an airy harem veil.

The old man was tall, a little stooped, his hair slate grey. He played with his eyes closed, his spare body swaying, seduced by the music. The Countess was taller than he was. Slim. Blonde. About thirty-five years old. She stared hard at Christine, her blue eyes cold, glistening, her red lips parted. Moist.

I don't remember what the girl was singing, only that it was beautiful, as irresistible as a hook in the mouth of a carp. I don't remember what she said to me after her scarf flew, red as a blood-gout, into the cold sea and I struck out into it, soaked to the skin in the freezing water. I remember the shape of her warm mouth as she spoke, twisting the sea-water out of the silk. I remember that her voice was silver. It did not matter what she said. To me, it was an invitation. I had earned her.

2.

I experienced her intensely for one week, I got to know the Countess and her frail father (even then it was obvious that he was not long for the earth), they always made me welcome in their large, immaculate home. The downstairs was decorated in the English Georgian fashion, all neo-classical pillars, ceilings lined with plaster laurel leaves, open-beaked eagles, the walls painted light blue, green, stark white. I wouldn't say I knew Christine.

This is not to say that she was not kind to me, or friendly. She may have even genuinely liked me. Certainly she acted as though she did. She couldn't have been miserable all that time we spent together in the attic among the bare dress-makers' dummies, headless as ghouls, all those veiled mirrors and obsolete furniture, all those soft, shrouded lurkers, listening as her father told us stories in his strange northern accent. *Little Lottie and the Angel of Music.*

I can hear him speaking now. A sweet voice that could be made rough or childlike depending on his need and the thrust of the story. He sat on an old leather trunk, pony-skin I believe, with patches of piebald fur missing. His large, precise hands moved as he spoke, as though he were conducting the narrative. Occasionally he scratched his moustache to hide a kind, sly smile.

'Little Lottie lived dreaming. The old fools in her village thought that she was a bad girl because she spent all her time singing, and some of the things that she sang were not very "proper", though they were all true.'

He stroked his daughter's hair with one huge hand, catching his fingers in her chocolate curls. The other hand he rested on my knee. I took this as a sign of his unconscious approval. I thought he thought that I was very fine. Probably he thought that I was a fool. All I wanted in the whole world was to lay my hands in those curls of hers, lose my nails in that dark river of hair. I thought she owed me that, at least, for rescuing her scarf, for condescending to adore her. I was very young.

The old man continued, 'Her father loved her very much and, since he was an artist himself, he knew that it is an easy lie of the common folk that artists have no morality. They have their own morality. They are dedicated to their truth, to portraying it as beautifully and powerfully as possible, even when it makes the small folk uncomfortable.

'Little Lottie lived a long time with her father in their safe little house at the edge of the forest. They were happy a long time, but happiness is not real if it lasts forever, and one day little Lottie woke to find her father burning in a fever, coughing blood into a rag.' The old man coughed here, wetly, into his handkerchief. I didn't know then that he was not acting.

'Before he died, he comforted the daughter he loved more than his own life. He said "Darling, do not be afraid. After I have made my home in heaven I will ask God the Father to send down to Earth the Angel of Music. He will sing to you in my voice and your art will improve until it glows from you like flame".'

'What happened then, Father?' Christine looked much younger than fourteen, leaning forward to him, her delicate hands digging into his knees, her eyes wide, gleaming with the sheen of tears.

The old man bent and kissed her once on her furrowed forehead, a move I longed to make myself. I would have killed to taste the salt of her skin.

He said, 'He died, daughter. It was very hard for Lottie, then. She grieved. But in time he kept his word. The Angel came. She sang better than she ever had before. She sang so well, in fact, that her people brought her to Paris and she became the greatest diva ever to sing in that great city. She ruled the stage for many years, and lived happily, so happily, ever after.'

And with that he ended the story. I went home, to my real home. It was time to take my place with my brother, learning the business. It was years before I learned what life gave Christine. I loved her image, faithfully, from a great distance. I never thought to write to her. In any case, it would not have been proper. At the time she was a member of the serving classes, though daughter of a great musician.

3.

Six years passed before I saw her again, my angel, my Christine. I never expected our reunion to come about in the way it did. My brother Philippe had been a patron of the Paris Opera since 1870 (the very year I met Christine). He continued his patronage when the opera company moved into the newly completed Palais Garnier after a long-delayed construction, interrupted by the famous siege of Paris. During that time of unrest and confusion several of the architects working under Garnier vanished in   circumstances that, given the war, were not very mysterious. They seemed much more violent later, those deaths, those hangings. When the dust settled and the torn corpses were cleared from the streets, the group of architects that attended the Master was found to have been reduced to one – Charles Garnier himself. It was no great loss, he said. The three whose bodies were found were hardly better than incompetent. The sole exception was the Mussliman whose corpse they never found, a man who had apparently travelled from the courts of the Shah in darkest Persia. The man who always wore a long-sleeved cashmere kaftan and his head draped with a keffiyeh that covered most of his oddly smooth face. My brother said that his loss was the only one Garnier really felt, and that the old architect grieved that they never found the body. He was, Garnier said, the only one with any real skill. My brother commented that Garnier's grief seemed oddly pronounced, as though he had lost a son and not an assistant.

In any case, Philippe had long been contented to sit on the sidelines of the theatre, courting his vague little dancer (He was always rather conventionally romantic, my brother.

He was the type who would have thought it daring to drink champagne from the toe of her smelly little shoe.) Philippe was deaf to every rumour of misfortune that haunted the cast almost from the time the doors opened, but my brother had a fixed idea of himself as a patron who could earn a profit. He funded the purchase of the contracts with a full quarter of the money that our father left him, and backed the managers he hired when they purchased the deed to the building itself.

Messieurs Firmin and Andre were two of a kind, both short dumpy men with a flair for the theatrical, as shown by their gleaming brushed beaver-top hats, bright scarves and elaborate, waxed mustachios. Their facial hair was so pointed, so hardened with wax, that they looked as though they had swallowed a pair of tiny bulls. Speaking to the one was, my brother said, exactly as good as speaking to the other. But they were dedicated to turning a profit and eagerly obeyed his commands, so they were tolerated.

The night that I returned to Paris (I had spent the last year on a ship learning the family business, accompanying reams of fabrics and spices from India) my brother welcomed me into his home, a massive, empty sprawl of bachelor opulence (his predilections betrayed by the filthy female undergarments strewn in the wash-chamber) and begged that I come out with him that night to enjoy the début of a new opera by Bizet.

'I know you'll enjoy it,' he said to me, forty years old, blond, bland and grinning like a schoolboy as we jostled forward in the coach, 'the composer has a soft-spot for gypsies and an earthy sensibility. You won't see La Carlotta in the lead role, unfortunately. There was, apparently, a misunderstanding regarding her contract. The new girl they've got in to replace her, Christina something, is very young, but supposedly good for the role. And her youth will be a boon to us. The role she's playing is apparently quite tempting. This *Carmen* has a lot of fire in it, a lot of amour. A lot of amour and very little dress. Nothing like a good young pair of nicely rounded … limbs filling out a delicate red garment. I expect to turn quite a profit with this show.'

I smiled in reply, not really considering. It had been so long since I'd seen Christine that the similarities in the names he'd mentioned (he'd got it wrong, of course) did not even stir up the ghost of a memory for me. I looked out of the window at the full streets, teeming as always with beggars and the growing ranks of the bourgeois – too poor at yet to afford their own coaches, but climbing quickly towards respectability – and thought of the sea.

After the greetings, canapés, the drinks, after that repulsive Giry woman led my brother, the managers and I to our box, after the curtain went up on the stage set to resemble a highly romanticised tobacco plantation, I became aware of the prickling of premonition. I felt the sweat pooling under my arms, forming beads like a diadem across my forehead. I *knew*, you see, that something was coming. She was. She did.

When she swept across that stage in the blood-brocade silk of a glamorous peasant, singing '*L'amour est un oiseau rebelle, que nul ne peut apprivoiser, et c'est bien en vain qu'on l'appelle, s'il lui convient de refuser. Rien n'y fait, menace ou prière; L'un parle bien, l'autre se tait, et c'est l'autre que je préfère; Il n'a rien dit mais il me plaît.*' in her provocative mezzo, while her fine white breasts trembled in her bodice and her pale, bare arms glistened in the lights, I was lost to myself, and to the world. I knew then that I must have her – no matter the cost.

My brother knew me very well; he had been young once himself. He offered to take me to see her in her borrowed changing room. She had not been the original diva (an understudy only). She would be after tonight. Philippe would call the painter in the morning to add her name to the star, blotting out 'La Carlotta' first. The intestines of the opera house were filthy for a place so recently opened, bare wood and plaster where the public mask was marble and gilt, but to me each splinter glowed and every rat was beautiful – though I must say that those dancers were far more attractive at a distance. Up close, they were all tired skin, bulging leg muscles, veins, and the stench of sweat. I feared the worst for Christine.

I needn't have bothered. There were voices in the room, male and female; I could hear them as we approached, although they were muffled. My brother knocked and the voices stopped. Christine Daaé opened the door, looking just a little older, still very much the luminous moon-girl, my long-limbed Artemis. She was alone in the room. The candle glowed gold behind her, reflected in the mirror, gold on her waist-long near-black curls.

She smiled at me, a small, sad lift of the lips, but did not appear to remember me at first. I had to remind her about our week on the seaside, her father, my brave rescue of her scarf.

I invited her to dinner that night. I can't remember what she said, but I know that she initially refused. I had to work hard to convince her. I could not understand why she would not accept me, why she withheld what I wanted. I knew that she wanted me, as I wanted her.

Eventually she acquiesced, with bitten lip and lowered eyes. I gave her a half-hour to change before I would come back to collect her. She withdrew demurely enough, care-fully latching the door. I was not offended by the sound of the lock. I turned back down the hall, softly singing her *Habanera* in my cracked voice, 'Love is a rebellious bird that none can tame, and it is well in vain that one calls it – if it suits him to refuse, nothing to be done, threat or prayer...'

CHRISTINE

4.

I studied at the smaller Theatre De Paris for nearly six years before the Palais Garnier opened and I finally found a chance to perform on stage as a singer. I grew from little more than a child in the filthy corridors of the old building, among the ropes, the defunct costumes, the ancient barre, polished by a thousand thighs, that the dance master brought from his previous theatre. If the hidden sections of the new theatre were as unsophisticated as the old, the facade the public saw fed my soul on a level of supreme sensuality that, I am certain, did me more harm than good. The Comte de Changy, I should say the *elder* Comte de Changy, took notice of me early – before I even began to be given singing roles. I am quite sure that if he had not brought me to the attention of the then managers, no one *else* would have noticed me, and I would have been a rat until the Countess, my patron, lost patience with (or interest in) my body and I would have found myself reduced to the same rough trade the other girls were used to.

None of that happened, as you can see. I *was* noticed. It became my duty to escort his bella La Sorelli to the post-production parties Firmin and Andre threw every evening for the Gentlemen who in truth sponsored the show by buying the boxes. After the final curtain came down, I would have time for a quick draught of cheap champagne (more vinegar than sweet) enough to kill the dust from the curtain, before quickly changing into one of my better frocks and rushing off to collect our beautiful, dear, our stupid Annie.

I changed among the other girls in a dark, clammy corner of the lesser rehearsal room. Compared to that dark space, Annie's cramped corner room was a palace. It was still new then, though this corner had been allowed to grow a little dusty in the years when building was abandoned. A cosy space, fur lined and bright with the glow of many whale-oil lanterns. She was a sweet girl, Annie, golden-haired and nicely plump. Actually, now that I think of it, she and the Comte shared a shade, in terms of their tresses. She was messy, cheerful, always ready to greet you with a smile and what a laugh she had! How she would howl – without always understanding the joke.

Sometimes, after a show, when she had danced particularly brilliantly, her bland face would cloud and she would suddenly begin weeping, freely, as shamelessly as a child. She could never name a reason for this. If you asked her, she would laugh, dash the tears from her eyes with one small, plump fist, and ask prettily for another glass of champagne to make her smile again.

It was my job to see that she was properly dressed for company, to escort her to the room to meet her lover and the other admiring gentlemen, and then to change the subject any way I could when her natural whimsy took a turn for the disgusting as it often might.

One night, while De Changy was speaking to his managers (this was, you remember, two sets of managers back) she started speaking to a tall, nearly skeletal man who had appeared, dressed in a cloak and dinner jacket, a fine fedora aslant, shadowing a face as bland and unlined as a new-born baby's. Her laughter had grown its most dangerous edge, the short hairs on my neck, cheeks, and arms rose in fear. La Sorelli was sweet, and she had a good heart, but her tongue could suddenly become impolitic and there were many investors present there this evening.

Annie and the stranger were standing at the point where the glorious stairs that make the Palais Garnier famous intersect and form an enormous marble Y, glittering in the light refracted in a thousand tear-shaped crystals that drip from the tremendous chandeliers and gaslight torches. Whoever he was, he stood terribly erect, his gloved hands hidden behind his narrow waist, clutching a fine ebony stick. My friend, who I was meant to be watching, was sloppily drunk, spreading her barely covered breasts against the wide, pink-veined bannister. I could not read his face as he looked at her, his features were oddly stiff, expressionless, but the arch of his body signalled contempt. I rushed to her side as quickly as I could, pleased that my new silk shoes did not slap against the carved stone stairs, pleased that I did not slip and crack my skull against the pavement.

I arrived in a rush, sweating a little, my breath panting, and took my friend by the arm. I began to apologise to the gentleman.

'I am sorry, monsieur.' Something in my tone must have startled him. He seemed to flinch at the sound of my voice, like the leg of the frog Papa showed me once, reanimated with unseen electricity stored in a battery. 'La Sorelli gets a little over-excited after performing. If you'll exc-'

'This is the gal I was talkin' bout, mister.' Annie slipped

her flabby arm around my neck so that I smelled her sweat and caking powdered perfume. She nodded her impudent head at the managers. 'They don't know it yet, but trust me, Christine can sing.'

He turned, whoever he was, and looked at me. I do not know if I can tell you what it is like to really be looked at, to feel a mind, alien to yours, attempting to bore beneath your skin and understand the composition of your true, your human bones. It is something that I am convinced few people ever experience. I looked into his odd yellow eyes (they looked like dead eyes, like the glazed, shrunken eyes of a fish left out too long in summertime) and I knew, suddenly, that the face I saw was no face at all. It was a mask.

'Is this true, girl? Can you sing?'

How can I describe his voice to you? It was a deep, sweet tenor, like rubbing raw, wet silk across my breasts. Seven words. They were delicious. I answered him.

'Yes. When I was a child. I haven't sung for years though, since my father died. I might have lost the gift.'

'No.' His voice was smiling, the painted lips never moved. 'The gift of music can never be taken from you. Is it possible that you simply require someone to sing to?'

My hands were clasped beneath my heart, I felt my own pulse in my fingers. I had totally forgotten about poor Annie. I never noticed when she slid to the floor.

The stranger nodded, as though to himself. 'It is possible. Probable. Yes.' His eyes flicked back to mine, a quick, cold cut given by a sharp, sure knife. 'Sing for me. Now.'

'Right here?' I looked around, the Comte and the managers were crowded in the lobby. They had moved on to brandy and fresh, expensive cigars. They might hear, but they would not interfere.

He nodded, his body unmoving, stiff as rigor mortis, his hands clasped hard behind his back.

I opened my mouth.

For the first time in years real music poured out.

He nodded once, bowing like someone unused to such motion, and left me there to scoop up Annie, who snored and drooled on to tiles that cost more per pound than her weekly salary. When I looked up again, staggering beneath the weight of her, he had totally vanished.

It is funny, now, how much loss I felt then. It felt just like an ending. It felt like a death.

5.

The Opera House is like Lazarus; a beautiful resurrected corpse shrouded in tarpaulins and plaster-dust, wood shavings that slowly lost their scent of pine and cedar, softening to mush. It lay entombed all those warring years while Father and I played and sang along the northern coasts, ignorant of the battling in cities. The theatre should have been abandoned. The basement is planted with bullets and corpse-bulbs, white skulls with hair roots the scenery assistants unearth while digging soil for the annual reprisals of Romeo and Juliet. More than a few real bones have been repurposed into scenery.

When I began my music lessons, high in the flies among the dangling pull-ropes, the Palais Garnier had just opened, but it had been an empty husk of itself for nearly a decade; I never encountered a place more ready for haunting. I have always been attracted to death. My father's stories painted it as the better part of life, the exit to a more beautiful existence, so things of the grave rarely repulsed me. I loved that new, old building as a kitten loves its cat.

As for the man who made me sing, nearly a year passed before I saw him again. No, I never saw him, but I heard his wonderful voice at our nightly assignations.

He arranged our lessons for me. Three days after our meeting on the stairs (when the memory of his strange, stiff body had begun to fade and I'd had time enough to question my judgement about his mask, his face) I found a letter waiting for me, tied with a strand of black ribbon and a wax seal impressed with the Lyre of Orpheus. He had slipped it, somehow, into my street shoes while I practised with the other dancers, one leg stretching on the barre.

The paper was yellowish, very fine, as though strands of silk were mingled in the fibres. The ink was good, thick, indelible as blood. The handwriting was terrible, as though a child had written it with matchsticks.

*Dear Miss Daaé
(or may I be so bold as to address you as 'Christine?'),*

The quality of your voice is undeniable, though currently undervalued. The management has, unfortunately, mistaken an unpolished diamond for a common river rock. Your drunken friend was right about you. In retrospect, I do not regret our conversation.

I know the look you have, the look of waiting. Patiently waiting for a promised visitor who has delayed and delayed until you begin to wonder if he is coming at all. My dear child, let me assure you (as your father did) that your wait will not be long. I will return to you everything that, in your innocence, you believe to be lost. I will begin with your song, scrape the earth from your voice and reveal the gem that has always be waiting.

> *It is more difficult than I can say for me to*
> *appear in the visible world. I am rather hard for*
> *the uninitiated to comprehend. Since it is appro-*
> *priate for angels to sing a little closer to heaven*
> *than the dowdy rehearsal rooms, meet me at eight*
> *in the evening on the scaffold supporting the main*
> *flies. I will see that Monsieur Bouquet has another*
> *engagement at that time.*
> *Do not expect to see me when you get there. It*
> *is no insult to you, dear child, to say that you are*
> *not ready to perceive me in the flesh.*
>
> *Until we meet again, I remain your*
> *Guardian Spirit*

On Monday night I mounted the flies, trailing the lace hem
of my second best frock in the dust. I expected, knowing
the habits of Mr Bouquet, a filthy slurry of rat dung and
chicken bones. Instead, like a miracle, the scaffold was laid
with a thick Persian carpet. There were silk cushions to rest
on in between scales, a music stand laden with notations, a
carafe of honey-sweetened water. The whole space was
bathed in light from five hand-shaped candelabra. They
were the gilt props from *The Haunted Manor*, painted plaster,
but the effect was regal enough.

We worked hard for many hours, though I did not realise
how long until after. Time passed like a dream. It was very
strange, for me, at first. His angelic voice seemed to spring
from three steps before me, but I seemed to feel a pair of
eyes on my spine. I soon grew used to it. I came to love my
lessons.

We met there for many months, until my first non-
chorus singing role when I was issued a room of my own.
He decorated. The rugs appeared, the cushions, and also a
small music box, mounted with a leaden monkey in red

silk robes. It played the cymbals when I wound the key embedded in its stiff spine.

The tag around its neck read, in his spidery hand, 'For a good daughter'.

Our lessons continued.

6.

We rarely conversed, hardly ever spoke of anything personal. He was very careful about that, whenever I would press for details about his life, if he had one, outside of my training he would state that he was working hard, making something for me. If I pressed any further the lesson would end in cold silence, and there I would be, sitting alone before the candle-lit mirror. He had a wonderful trick of making it seem as though my own reflection were speaking from that simple, frameless bit of glass. I knew, of course, that he was really somewhere behind me, but he asked me never to seek for him and I respected that. I was getting a great deal out of these lessons and I wanted them to continue. It took months for him to even tell me his name. He never let it slip until he met me underground. He preferred 'Master'. As my teacher, it was his right and perfectly proper.

And yes (let me be honest now, if only to myself, to this book) his voice did sometimes sound very like my father's. Usually when he let something about his carefully papered-over past slip. A mention of his childhood with the nuns, made while explaining to me the importance of empathy in storytelling (and singing is storytelling) or a few words about his hatred of carnivals – a funny trait, I thought, for an accomplished ventriloquist – would roughen his voice.

More often he sounded, frankly, as though he had swallowed Father's ancient violin. It stirred me in a way I found delicious and disturbing. His voice made me think of that story my father told me, of the daughter who sang so beautifully and died so young. Her father grieved so hard for her that God took pity and placed her voice into his fiddle so that every time he played, she sang for him.

I wondered if such miracles could happen in reverse, like writing reflected in a glass. I wondered if a voice I loved, a soul I clung to, could sing to me from another throat.

So yes, we were intimate, sometimes unintentionally. Yes, I did love him, what I knew of him. His shadows. His scraps. I loved what he did for me. My love was innocent then, at least of touch. It felt so good to have someone who could be proud of me. But my invisible Master could be strange, too. When I began scooping roles he promised always to watch me perform from the best box in the house. He used those carnival tricks to secure the plush darkness, those wonderful acoustics for himself, without wasting a dime beyond his always generous twenty-franc tip to Meg's mother, Madame Giry, who was in charge of seating and survived on her tips.

According to Madame Giry he made the walls weep blood (like something from one of the Countess' countless gothic novels) and, in time, the musicians who hit their notes flat and the clumsiest dancers suddenly began disappearing. I heard Little Meg and La Sorelli cracking dark jokes about carrying knots made out of segments of hangman's rope to ward off murderous ghosts.

They might not have been murders, I thought, not all of them. The house inspector rarely found bodies. Besides, what kind of killer targets the untalented?

But he was strange after the offensive members had been cut off. He would laugh more, during our lessons. Mad, joyful laughter that seemed to leap from flame to flame between the fixtures I kept gleaming with an oil-soaked rag. If he did not kill them himself, God owed him a favour.

Things continued in this vein for several months, before the Comte's little brother, the boy from the beach, crashed into my rooms and unsettled what I took for my happiness.

ERIK

4.

Master Garnier and I made it across the manicured court-yard (lush palms, figs, that troublesome fountain with the spouting dolphins that I had designed so well then watched that idiot of a foreman destroy with his heavy hand at plumbing) to the building site. We arrived at the same moment that the half-naked labourers were completing their midday meal of fried, spiced dough balls and ground chickpeas. My master went to rouse them from their meal while I walked back to the site. The foreman, as usual, was nowhere in sight.

We had been working in this sandy patch of earth for nine months and the struggle to see my structure rise from my perfectly planned designs was more than tedious. I'd had no idea, in the beginning, how many things could run foul in such a job of construction.

Yesterday, for example, the labourer who looked like he had taken a year-long break between changing loincloths (their stench was terrible – even to me) dropped a sculpture I'd made at the Shah's special request; a figure of a woman done in soft lead, whose face belonged to the ruler's favourite concubine. I had to guess at the body, but I had captured the face perfectly. I found out, much later, that he had broken several strong local taboos allowing me, an unrelated male (even such a specimen of the gender as I am) to look upon a woman he owned. I based the naked body (it was too erotic to be termed a 'nude') on the rather fleshy Eve I saw in Master Garnier's miniature reproduction of the Sistine Chapel. To me, the shoulders seemed like they would better fit a cricketer, but the Shah had revealed to me that he liked his women large.

In any case, it was a beautiful piece of sculpture. I meant to mount it to the top pillar in the new main bathhouse. The coolie was supposed to be securing it to the waiting marble base. I rather suspect that he dropped it on purpose, in protest at my (not the Shah's) display of bad taste and general immorality. This assumption was not baseless – I had caught him, several times, peering between the curtains that served as doors in my rooms. Perhaps he thought the strange white devil would have a demon's face. He wouldn't be far wrong.

The painted lead deformed as he dropped it, the fine face flattened out until it resembled a mask more of horror than lust. I could not repair it. I'd lost the original wax likeness when I cast the metal. I resigned myself to risking the Shah's displeasure by asking for another forbidden audience with his lady, in his chambers.

I could happily have slaughtered that idiot, morally pretentious coolie. I was busily, half-seriously, contemplating my options for corpse-disposal while my eyes stared at the divot her face had dug in the delicate imported tile. I have the gift of partitioning thoughts and while I was picturing the various torments that I could give to the goon who ruined my sculpture another part of my mind worried about how I could possibly repair that harsh crack in the floor. I gave equal weight to both problems and I had found some fitting solutions when suddenly a breeze blew through the half-completed walls and sent sand seeping through the seams of my mask. This was too much! The pain was intolerable, adding another layer of irritating grit to my already pus-blooming cheeks.

I had to take the mask off, cleanse myself before I bled through the kid skin and my weakness was made visible to all.

Luckily I was alone, I thought, in the bathhouse. The pools had not been filled as yet, but there was water everywhere in pitchers and half of the mirrors I'd made were already mounted on the walls. I took my opportunity.

My foreman took his.

My mask slid off like a glove, issuing a small shower of sand, revealing the bandages that I had earlier applied. I was busily unwinding the gauze, my vision totally blocked, when I felt four hands grasp me by the arms and shoulders.

'Faugh!' I heard a voice I knew, speaking in Arabic, a language I'd learned on the six-month journey to the palace, 'It's like grasping at a rotted toad.'

The hands clamped all the tighter for wanting to let go. I tried to scream, only to feel my mouth filled with wood, a bar to bite down on. My foreman spoke in rough accents, 'I know, my friend, but think of the gold.'

I tried to fight as they peeled away the last of my gauze. I am very strong, much stronger than I look, but they had me securely. I was helpless as they saw my shame.

'My god, it's a living corpse. You were right about the stench … this jinn will bring us better than a few old coppers.'

My former foreman smiled with his toothless gums, ripping my robes to reveal my poor flesh, so that he held my naked form. 'Yes, but first we must get it to our buyers. I can't do that, if I have to look at it.'

Had I been free, I would have bitten his nose off. At least I had the teeth to do the job. It might have improved his disposition.

That was when they bundled my stripped body into that burlap sack. The rough fibres peeled my skin like an onion so that the fabric felt slicked with my brownish-red blood. I began to feel myself letting go of myself and found a brief relief in madness.

5.

I do not know how long the journey lasted, the days slid into one another, differentiated only by subtle differences in light and motion (the movement of the sack I was suspended in seemed to slow in darkness – it never stilled). The heat was unmitigated. I cannot describe what it was like to be suspended for so long in that scabbed chrysalis. My skin has always been delicate, fragile; it scraped off in strips like the half-solid rind that forms on cool cream soup. Days of beating sun spoiled the tatters so that I smelled like the corpse of the evil king in the Book of Judges who Ehud stabbed through the bowels. Say what you will about those Sisters, my time with the nuns proved useful in the end – if only through providing me with metaphors.

My mouth dried, my eyes ached, parching in my skull; they felt raw and dry through closed lids. My temples throbbed and my throat ached with the acid residue of vomit. I only lived because some member of the party at whose mercy I was travelling decided that it would be more profitable to deliver living cargo to their clients, and not a desiccated mummy. Once a day I felt the joy of water as someone poured a bucket of brackish washing water over the burlap which encased me. This action also provided me with my first clue about my method of transport. The stench of wet camel is unmistakable.

I do not know if I was still held captive by my foreman and his coolie; I suspect not. They would want to clear themselves of suspicion – Garnier, at least, would be looking for me. The Shah might seek me out as well. He would not wish to leave his stately pleasure drome in unfinished ruins. No one else could satisfactorily complete it. No, the foreman probably sold me on that very evening, allowing a travelling merchant to take a cut of his profit in return for allowing him to show himself bright and early at the work site, clearing himself of suspicion and adding his regular pay-cheque to his other illicit takings.

In any case, the foreman was not present when the journey ended. I felt myself lifted from the camel, still encased in the sack. I heard a rough voice, bellowing curses in Spanish, saying, 'Ay Dios Mio, what a stench! Are you sure it is not dead? We don't pay for corpses, Mr Chinky.'

Another voice, disgruntled, answered. 'If you don't believe me, give it a kick. It will whimper for you.'

I knew enough to wriggle before the Spaniard took him up on it. I moved very lightly, knowing well enough by then that I was no butterfly, that this pupa could never be shed by my own power. My strength was greatly reduced by starvation.

I had the dubious pleasure of listening to their laughter, and hear the familiar clink of gold as someone exchanged my body for his coins. I heard the grunts and sputters of a camel being mounted, heard the crash of whip on hide, and then I was dragged, mercifully, out of the beating sun and into some shade.

'Let's see what I've bought, then.' The Spaniard knelt above my bag; I felt his shadow severing the light. 'Don't move more than you must, or I'll add to your ugliness with my blade.'

He drew a section of the burlap taut and pierced it with a long, curved knife. It was the first solid thing that I had seen in several days. It looked so beautiful, so powerful, shining. I imprinted on it like a duck fresh from the egg. He widened the hole, using his enormous rough hands to tear the slit. I spared a thought of pity for his wife, his animals.

He drew me out by the shoulders, cursing and gagging as he freed my bloody body from the sack. *'Santa María, Madre de Dios, ruega por nosotros, pecadores, ahora y en la hora de nuestra muerte.'* He left my body on a pile of straw and turned away to vomit, looking at me long enough to say, 'I was not cheated. Creature, you live, and you're guaranteed to terrify the marks.'

I was too weak and angry to reply to this. It was all I could do to lie gasping in the straw. I felt like a fish, dying in a creel among the dried waterweed. Luckily, he did not appear to need any help in conversation. He continued, brushing my blood on to his poorly cured leather trousers and using those same filthy fingers to straighten his vest, 'The only question, as I see it, is are you too ugly? Will you fascinate as well as horrify?'

I glared at him, noticing for the first time that the straw I lay on was piled in the centre of a garish-painted tiger cage. I was already a captive. He was standing now, supporting his bearish bulk on one of the rusted iron bars. He nudged me with the cracked toe of his black boot. 'You are always naked? Do you ever wear clothes?'

I pushed myself up on to my elbows. It was all I could manage. Almost all. I spoke to him in my own language, 'I have been accustomed to fine garments, Monsieur. I regret that you do not see me at my best at this moment.'

'It speaks. French! And in an educated accent.' His grin was wide, leering. 'Your *garments* (as you say) will hardly be fine here, but I will see that you have something to cover yourself with. After all, there will be ladies in our audience. Some of them young, and too innocent to be traumatised by that thing between your legs.' He stooped to look closer. Had I any strength, I would happily have killed him. 'One part of you is man, at least.'

He laughed again, spat over his left shoulder. On his way out the door I asked for food to eat, water to drink and wash myself with.

'You will have food enough, I'm sure. I sell vegetables and other things for the crowd to throw, and as for water, I will bring some. You may wash, or drink. Really, I hope that you will drink. A wild man, a primordial monster, should stink a little.'

He was as good as his word. That night the gates of the carnival opened and the crowds came in. I endured a hell that I never thought that I could speak of. It cost me something to survive as long as I did, something valuable that I am sure I will never recover. I was lucky to escape with my mind.

It was seven years before I met my master again, though I had long since finished thinking of him in those terms. He wandered, by chance, into the carnival as we cruised the coast of Nice after a four-year tour of Italy. Wandering through the lines of cages, jostled by the crowds, he recognised my voice at once. I was sitting in a pile of dross on the floor of my cage (it had never been cleaned, there were bones everywhere) dressed in a tattered brown loincloth. It had once been white. My face was exposed, but Monsieur Garnier had never been made to look at it. He would have had no reason to recognise me if I had been silent. I had not seen myself in years, but when I could think lucidly I felt the scars and pustules and knew that I was worse.

I was singing a song that the nuns had taught me long ago, *'Au clair de la lune mon ami Pierrot prête-moi ta plume pour écrire un mot ma chandelle est mort. Je n'ai plus de feu ouvre-moi ta porte pour l'amour de Dieu.'*

'Erik?' I looked up into his fat, wide-eyed face. I did not know him, but the word he spoke itched at my brain like a phrase in a forgotten language. 'Erik? My God, lad, is it you?'

I could not move; such shame filled me, such deep terror. I sat there, trembling in filth. He spoke to me softly, until I calmed enough to remember my life and tell him of my troubles, of my betrayal at the hands of our former foreman. It all returned to me as I spoke, along with a rising sensation of resentment that he, of all people, should find me like this! I was silent, my song departed.

Knowing that our time was brief, I hurried in my narrative, speaking as clearly as I could, clutching the bars with my hands which he touched, once, giving as much comfort as he could stand. He knew that it hurt me terribly to speak. Still, his eyes slid from my face.

I was used to baring my visage to the air, I knew how terrible it was, how the youngest children cried at the sight of it while the adolescents hurled their gobs of wilted lettuce wrapped around round apples of horse dung. How the men came from farms and dockyards to compare the hard part-healed lesions on my face to particular pieces of female anatomy. I was used to the way the young women either covered their nostrils with squares of perfumed silk and hurried past, or gawped up at me like over-bred hens drowning in a rainstorm, beginning to laugh after the horror-blanche had fled their faces and the nervous laughter bubbled up.

I'd made a lot of money for my owner. His investment paid off.

Garnier left quickly, almost as soon as I had finished speaking, after slipping me a knife so that I might slice free my wire-bound fingers. My hands were always fastened to make eating more difficult and increase the spectacle of my 'act'. The padlocks on the door were filled with lead solder; when Garnier returned that night he brought a pair of strong bolt-cutters that sliced the lead like butter. We escaped without incident, disturbing neither dogs nor big the bull elephant that slept in its chains, and I spent the remainder of the year recovering in the sane, ivy-covered villa where Garnier rested between projects. I made a new mask, acquired new bearings, planned. There were vineyards on the property and I walked them, pacing the rows in my new tailored suits, learning the craft. At night I caught up on my music composition and architectural studies. The lush rococo forms I favoured were coming into vogue and I knew that with the right commission I could earn a lot of money while fulfilling a long-held, treasured dream combining both my prime interests. I took up boating for a while, early in the morning. I loved it then, when the world was quiet. I developed a taste for the sea.

6.

It seems to the world that politics and art are joined masters. Certainly, if one wishes to advance in the world, one must be seen to bow to convention. I will not bow, and my face was not made to wear a simper, so it would seem that my desires were doomed to be thwarted. This was not so. I paid a steep price to survive my life in the cage. Something vital was burnt out of me (and I was only half-human to begin with – I have not much spare) but something also was gained. My will was hardened. Even Monsieur Garnier acknowledged this change in me and expressed it in our relations. The former-Master became my mask, facing the world with his form and voice but strictly adhering to my decisions.

When Emperor Napoleon III decided that he wished to commission a new opera house he cleared 12,000 square metres of land on the site of his own choosing, in a green space, surrounded by many ancient, graceful trees and a few modern buildings. The Emperor himself opened the floor to submissions from architects, deciding who won on the strength of the plans. Of course I sent him my design. The signature said 'Charles Garnier' in his own fine copperplate hand, but the drawings were mine. He was known, after all, and much more affable in conversation. He presented the blueprints before the throne.

There was never a question that we would be victorious. The Empress, I heard, had something to say about it. Charles reported to me that she greeted him in the gilded reception hall, saying, 'What is this? It's not a style; it's neither Louis Quatorze, nor Louis Quinze, nor Louis Seize!'

Always the politician, knowing that our sponsor was

within earshot, my master grinned down at her (the lady was buried beneath a wig that would have fitted out fifteen bald brunette maidens) and said, 'Why Ma'am, it's Napoléon Trois, and you're complaining?!' Oh how I laughed to hear that!

In any case, we won, and I was hired (along with three incompetents) as an 'assistant' to the architect. The public thought that I was meant to do odd jobs, to micro-manage, supervising the building on a menial level. This was exactly what I wanted. I could run around the site shrouded in the Persian robes I adopted and speaking in an accent, moving fast and silent on my long spider-legs, sneaking up on the workmen and ensuring that they scrimped on no part of the construction. None of the sculpted nudes which garnished this roof would experience the horror of a smashed, disjointed face.

Before construction began, I built a better mask. Painted wax above a chamois-lined mould made to fit my own strange features. I sculpted it in the style of a young, handsome pantomime rake with cherry red lips, full, coloured cheeks, and comfortable eye-holes. When I wore my sleek black wig above my scabrous skull the result was positively striking, and quite effective, provided no one attempted to come too close. As far as I know, it worked. Though, even then, there were rumours of a ghost.

The months became years as the walls rose up. The plain brick first, a skull to support the thin marble skin I made to face the world. Then the columns, the fine nude statuary with their full, luscious figures, the fine copper domes decorating the centre of the roof and the four corners, a design I borrowed from the palace of the Shah and softened for a Western audience. I supervised the construction of the foyer, lined with marble, spaces for the mirrors that I intended to fill the room with later.

The enormous Y-shaped marble staircase leading to the boxes, the centrepiece of my foyer, was half-finished when the Franco-Prussian war broke out and the city was sieged. The entirety of the national economy was diverted into war. Garnier and I continued construction, for a while, at our own expense. I made cuts where I could, in labour, not materials, beginning with the three sub-architects whose work had never pleased me well and who were largely untraceable once I laid their bodies on the soft soil of the unfinished basement. I fully intended to return and cover them, later.

We continued working in this way for a few months. Garnier and I woke each morning at four and remained at the site, hauling blocks and laying masonry as one with our minimal crew, but it could not continue. Eventually even our crippled message-boy was taken for the national guard. The city was besieged. Water and food were limited. We could not escape the gates of the town, we could not continue with the construction of the building. There was fighting in the streets.

I felt as though I were in a cage again, as though God Himself were thwarting me. I began, in anxiety, peeling the white flesh from the beds of my fingernails, until the blood flowed. I could focus on nothing, not even composing music, the passion that used to fill my nights.

I spent one entire week in bed, rising only to visit the facilities. I would not open the bedroom door, no matter how poor Charles hammered at it. When I rose from my bed at the end of this time, I was famished and my mind was filled with a tremendous, unspeakable clarity. I felt cleansed and resolved.

I wrote dear Monsieur Garnier a letter which I left prominently displayed on my favourite drafting desk, packed a large trunk and two valises with equipment and clothes (my strength rushed back to me in freedom like a river swollen by the thaw – I carried them easily) and vanished through the window into darkness to take my refuge in the basement of the Opera House I dreamed of, the seat of my defeat.

I lived there, quite happily, for some time while bullets flew and bodies fell above my head. I bought my food from the night market where my mask was never noticed and spent my days at my desk, designing fancies that I never expected the universe to see. It was strange, I could live with a ruined life – so long as the ruins were glorious. Mediocrity was and is a bane to me. This failure, being prominent, was something of a balm to my wounded soul.

Imagine my surprise when I found that after nearly five years and the fall of the Emperor, construction on my Opera House began in earnest once more, with my old friend Garnier at the helm! Of course, he assumed that I was long since dead. He grieved for me as he would have for his child, had he had one. I did not disabuse him. He had suffered enough on behalf of a friend. Besides I was a ghost by now; the Opera Ghost was what the little dancers called me. They build a fine mythology around what they thought of as my head. I helped them do it. Little things vanished, the less-talented members of the orchestra suffered minor accidents (a twisted ankle, a mysterious burn) until their places were filled with a minimum of competence. Occasionally I allowed myself the luxury of murder. I took care of that butcher who twisted the flies so that the scenery dropped at the wrong time, or rolled up in a flurry. All in all, the shows were better with the Ghost.

And all the while, in the darkness, in my underworld home, my own opus, the heart of my life, began to form, notes on white paper, seeking only a focal point, a theme to bring it whole into the world.

I have always been drawn to genius. Most of the girls were fine little fripperies, pretty enough, sweet to look at and listen to, minimally skilled. Only one shone with the sheen and weight of true gold in a pile of brass. Christine Daaé. It was my duty as a fellow artist to train her, to ready her to take that place of prominence that had so long been denied me. I found out all I could about her, listening in to conversations, questioning kind-hearted Madame Giry (a good source of information for one with the means to give adequate tips). She answered more freely than I would have expected, considering that my voice seemed to emerge from her lantern. Of all the opera staff, she alone seemed unafraid of the Ghost.

I uncovered Christine's current living situation, mourned for her when I learned about the death of her father, insinuated my way into discovering her goals. I found the ideal way to motivate her. She was not perfect, underneath the image of the muse beat the heart of a wild, passionate girl who could tantrum and storm with the best of them (not that I ever knew many), but her gifts were true and I must foster them. When the time came, I arranged an appropriately accidental meeting.

You might well ask if it was only a sense of fellow-spirit that drew me to her, not that there is ever any 'only' when it comes to human sympathy. Let me assure you, sincerely: it was innocent, at first. I would have worked so hard for her if she had been born ugly. Unfortunately, she was not.

RAOUL

4.

When I returned to Christine's dressing room, arriving to the minute at the time I appointed, she didn't reply to my knock. When I tried the door I found it unlocked, my target vanished. Without her slight form filling the room with her numinous light, it was a shabby space, garbed in theatre baubles. The costumes that looked so rich and fine from the stage were revealed on the hanger to be cheap reworkings of scavenged finery, of the fast-fastening, loosely hooked sort that a street-walking prostitute would purchase in the hopes of raising their prospects by seducing a gentleman high in standing and poor of eyesight.

I knew, logically, that these garments, this German shepherdess costume for example, were intended to allow for a swift change in the aisles, but I still felt rather taken in by her, used. I told myself that my love, though new, was pure and that Christine was cast from higher quality – not just brass overlaid with gold, unlike those tacky hand-shaped candlesticks she'd left lit before her mirror.

Well, if she could not manage our assignation, perhaps she had a good reason. I knew that I had no right to go poking through her things, her personal belongings, but I considered that her desk was considerably cluttered with paperwork and those cheap tallow candles were guttering rather low. I should extinguish them for her, stopping a house-fire was the least I could do. Besides, she might have left me a note.

I moved into the room, imagining an oddly wordless love-note (the letters scrawled across the delicate paper my mind created were meaningless, but the hand was girlish, looping, and their intent was clear) intending to snuff the flames quickly between my forefinger and thumb, after a quick look for the letter I hoped and suspected was there.

The desk was covered in cosmetics, glass perfume bottles, a tortoiseshell box of lavender powder, rouge for lips and cheeks, kohl to enhance her onyx eyes and make them visible from stage. All of this was delightfully feminine, perfect for the girl of my dreams, and it all smelled wonderful. There were also a few rolled scripts for upcoming productions. *Faust. Romeo and Juliet.* The new production, that raucous, enchanting *Carmen* that débuted tonight. As for that last, I had no idea what the critics would say about it, nor did I particularly care. I was certain that they would not dare to criticise Christine. She was absolutely perfect.

I shifted them aside, forcing the scripts behind an ugly wind-up monkey doll that her father must have given her, and there were her letters, underneath, where any fool could find them. I sat down in her chair, a delicate Queen Anne with thin ebony arms, and began reading the envelopes.

There was nothing for me.

Most of the letters were addressed to her, and written in various female hands. Some were educated, others not; they all had one thing in common, that feminine slant which betrays that gender's inherent weakness of mind – a trait the stronger gender has generously decided to find a charming focus for our love.

One letter was different. The envelope was blank, but the seal was arresting. It was some sort of stringed instrument, a harp or lyre impressed in black wax; appropriate I thought, for the daughter of a famous violinist. Perhaps it was an old message from her father, a memento she had kept close, like the ugly monkey, for sentimental reasons.

I only opened it because I thought that it would draw us closer. I wanted to know what the father was like, to better know the spirit of the girl. I never dreamed the trouble it would cause us.

It began:

Dearest Christine,

You will never know the joy I feel, hearing you sing so beautifully, knowing that you have agreed to use your voice, your tremendous talent to serve my purposes. It stirs me to know that I have the pleasure of nurturing your intellect, your vast musical skills, so that with love and training your genius will grow...

I crumpled the letter in my fist, shaken by a sudden bout of rage. The blood pounded in my temples, throbbed against my skull so hard that it felt as though my eyes would burst inside their sockets. I had to bite my tongue to stifle my screams.

Answering to an impulse that I cannot explain, I tore my nails from my palms and looked up into the mirror. I saw there a version of my usual face: the same soft skin, the same wide blue eyes that I saw this morning. My features were as regular and pleasing as ever, if a bit pale. My eyes were a bit red about the rims, my new blond moustache could use a small trim — these were the only visible flaws. I said to myself, 'Whoever he is, he cannot match me. I will win her yet. With my charm, with my love. Wait, Raoul. Wait and see.'

I was almost ready, almost cleansed enough to read the rest of the letter (I had smoothed the admirably expensive paper against my left knee) when I heard a gentle knocking on the frame of the door, followed by a small, high gasp that sounded as though it had come from the throat of a child. I turned in the chair, half rising, and saw a young girl I thought I recognised, one of the dancers, still dressed for the stage.

She was a thin, dark thing with a face that would have been beautiful if the cheeks had not been so sunken, giving her a look that was both young and old, half maiden, half crone. She asked, 'Who are you? What are you doing here? This is Christine's room.'

Her voice was very rough and she had a lisp that was quite understandable to me once I saw that her tongue had nothing to strike against, finishing her letters. In her mouth 'Christine' elongated to 'Chrisseen'.

My mind, an untrained animal, flashed on filthy alleyways, the pleasures found in foul places, to the soft pressure of a silk-lined hole. I responded, 'I'm a friend of hers. I've known her for years.' I fully rose, placed the letters, carefully, back on the table. 'The lady who orders the boxes told me that I would find a letter for me here. I came only to collect it. Unfortunately, she was wrong.' I spread my empty hands. 'As you can see, there is none.'

Her forehead furrowed. In a gesture that was utterly laughable she spread her legs to fill the door, crossing her thin arms across the place where, if she was lucky, breasts would eventually grow. 'My mother said that?' She shook her head, her hair (light, so light against that skin) went flying. 'No, no Monsieur. She would never do such a thing. If there was a letter, she would have given it to you herself. You must be mistaken. I must ask you to leave.'

I smirked at her, a grimace that I attempted and failed to transform to warm smile. 'If I am to leave, you will have to let me pass you.'

She started a bit at that, but drew back, into the room, so that I had to almost touch the filthy fringe of her skirt as I slid through the door. I tried to pass her a five-franc note, 'For honest silence'. She would not take it. It fell from my hand to the floor.

Ah well, I thought, it will not harm her to save her pride while I am here. She will pick it up later. My secret is secure.

Somewhere in the empty theatre a clock bonged the hour. I was twenty minutes late to meet my brother. Tonight I would eat well, converse with my elders, and plan my tomorrows. If there was a rival for her love, I would defeat him. The challenge would add sweetness to the conquest. I felt my cup to be supremely full.

I hurried out into the night, joining the party as they entered their carriage. Behind me, in an empty room, candles blazed before the mirror. Wax melted until the flames guttered. The room was in darkness.

5.

My brother and I rode to the restaurant with the managers, Andre and Firmin. My brother's managers were surprisingly boisterous for such unassuming men, pouring cognac for their fat, nearly identical wives (one was in blue, the other acid green, but their hair and faces were as similar as their husbands' and I couldn't tell to whom they belonged). My sullen silence went largely unnoticed amidst all the joy at Christine's luminous success as the tempestuous Spanish Gypsy.

The dancer that they called La Sorelli was already well on her way to drunkenness by the time I entered the cab. Her sleeves had fallen halfway down her fair, round arms and her hair was wild, as though the crows had been at it for nesting material. My brother did not seem to notice. He was far too busy staring down her gaping blouse. Not that she minded, she was hanging from his arm in a way that I found quite shocking.

Looking at them, the middle-aged man, the whorish dancer, I was filled with disgust. They called that love? It was nothing like what I had for Christine. That was pure, true, as perfect as she was. Nothing this gross assemblage had could compare with it. I must endure this evening, then turn my resources to winning her.

We had reserved the finest seats in Le Chat Noir, a long oak table inlaid with ivory and laid with exquisite linen, and we arrived at a little after eleven. We were still supping at midnight, Monsieur Firmin had broken free a splinter of lamb bone and was using it to pick his teeth clean while one of the women spooned cream and vivid red liqueur into her mouth from her dish of mixed fruits. She had spilled the syrup across the silk ruching that crossed her broad bust like the scales of a serpent.

I had eaten next to nothing, having no appetite. My confidence was an oscillating thing, as it often is for the young.

I endured three long hours of mandatory celebration, time I spent drinking far too much absinth without any sugar to ameliorate the bitterness, and speaking to no one if I could avoid it. By the time we returned to my brother's house I was tired and irritable, more than ready to retire. We said goodnight to each other almost as soon as we entered the door. I had heard him order his driver to deliver his woman back to her rooms, but I suspected that was a ruse. As soon as I was safely out of ear-shot, I knew that the carriage would cycle round again and regurgitate the whore into my brother's waiting arms.

I gritted my teeth, hard, at the thought of it.

In my well-appointed room, surrounded by the rich finery of leather and brass, I slept badly. I tossed and turned on my pillow, assaulted by nightmares, by visions of her, my goddess. Mine at last. In dreams I embraced her: as I had desired since childhood, I held her close and kissed her mouth only to find, as my tongue tasted the nectar of her lips, that she rotted like fruit in my arms. I saw her beautiful face pucker like a spoiled apple, her eyes liquefy and sink back into her skull, so that she became the very bride of living death, smiling at me, approaching (with bared white teeth) my fragile human neck.

I woke to daylight, yellow butter melting through the curtains. There was the smell of sweet bread, buttered rolls, fresh, hot coffee. The maid approached my covered body, bearing a tray and a note written on a single sheet of linen paper, folded once.

It was unsealed, marked only with my name in a firm

calligraphic hand that was educated, almost masculine. I opened it, my heart fluttering as I sipped my scalding coffee.

Dear Raoul,

Of course I remember the boy who brought me back my favourite scarf. If I was rude to you last night, it is only because you appeared so unexpectedly. I would be glad to renew our acquaintanceship, but as you know, I am an artist. I would like, one day, to be a great diva. Since that is the case, and since my work must be focused on attaining my goal, everything else (even friendship) must come second.

If this is amenable to you, I would be happy to see you for tea sometime next week. You may call at the home of Countess Marie De Vinci any afternoon save for Sunday. She will be happy to welcome you. You knew my father well, I believe. It would be good to speak with someone who shared that experience.

Do not expect to speak with me over the next several days. I will be travelling to Brittany to pay my respects at the grave of my father, after which I will return to the O.H. to reprise my Carmen. Thank you for your compliments on my performance. It is a difficult and fulfilling role. I have much work to do to perfect it.

Your Sincere Friend,
Christine Daaé

You will never know what joy I felt when I read those words. She was glad to see me! She wanted to renew our 'acquaintanceship', she remembered me with joy!

The terrors of the night were blown away in an instant. I sat up in bed with a whoop of mad joy, tore my nightdress free, tearing the buttons and forgetting the presence of the uniformed maid (who gasped in her shock). I dressed in a hurry. Suddenly, I knew exactly what I must do. Christine was my own, and soon I would be with her.

I had a train timetable in the top drawer of my desk, I glanced at it, laughing. A train to Brittany departed in two hours. I would make it if I hurried.

6.

After my rushed breakfast, I hurried through a palaver with Philippe as I half-explained my destination. He kept me with him longer than was either comfortable or strictly necessary, out of some misplaced sense of brotherly cama-raderie.

'An assignation with a lady! Of course you cannot keep her waiting, lad.' He smiled warmly up at me, comfortable in bed. A small white hand emerged from a lump in the thick coverlet, stroked his greying stubble. He batted the birdlike fingers back out of sight, as though I had not noticed.

My brother leaned out through the heavy drapes, spilling his expanding gut over the edge of the mattress as he rifled the drawers of his bedside table. I should have been content to leave a note.

'Ah, here we are.' His grin was wide and condescending as he handed me his second best purse, heavy with gold. 'Show her a good time, boy. Travel safe.'

I bit back my impatience (imagine the nerve of it! He acted exactly as though I were a child seeking an allowance!) and forced a thankful smile. I left him there, with his 'lady'. I assume he was able to amuse himself. His bed was occupying, and occupied, enough.

By the time I flagged down a cab (I was unwilling to wait for Alphonse to ready Philippe's personal rig) I was in a fluster of anxiety. I knew that Christine would not be in Brittany long. There were other performances later in the week and as the leading lady she would have to sing. I calmed myself with the thought that a trip to the coast took many hours and there were not many trains. She would remain there one night, at least. She wanted to arrange a mass for her father (an act that filled me with joy: a dutiful daughter will make a dutiful wife!) and such things take time. Most villages only have one morning service. Probably she was seated, right at this moment, in the priest's office, paying the appropriate fee and filling in the paper-work.

Or else she was kneeling, right now, above her father's sunken grave. I wondered, would there be a gravestone or would he have to lie content beneath a wooden cross? He was poor in life, but his progeny had been adopted by a Countess. Christine would inherit a title, in time.

I thanked God for the Countess, for taking Christine into her family, an act that made this courtship possible. But then who could fail to love a girl as perfect as she was?

I glanced out of the window, saw the streets, the city's intestines, fall fast behind me. I saw, like a dream, a ragged man on the cobbles reach out to a passing woman in 'respectable' dress. She might have been a baker's wife. I could not tell if her hands were gloved with cloth or grains of flour. The man, a very ugly specimen of the lower classes, had a goitre on his cheek the size of a hen's egg. I saw, in an instant, the way he grabbed her purse, snapping the silver-tone chain of her chatelaine.

I thought of signalling the driver to stop, but then remembered the train, and the invisible rival who would steal my treasure, and let my hand drop. Right now, for me and my future happiness, every second counted.

Thirty minutes later we arrived at the station. I had missed the early train by a full five minutes. I would have to wait for the evening departure and travel at night. Luckily, there was a cafe at the station. I bought a coffee, brandy-spiked, a roll with ham, and sat down at the table to eat, smoke, and read the daily newspaper.

Carmen had been reviewed. The critic did not care for the opera, he thought it was 'common', but I blushed with pride to see three full paragraphs dedicated to the glory of Christine.

CHRISTINE

7.

I sang my first leading role in spring, a début by Bizet that I loved from my first glance at the score. That composer did something wonderful with folk music, took the simple-seeming tunes and reels of the so-called 'common folk' and brought them, blooming, into complex art. I hadn't heard anything like it since those long-ago days when my father improvised with Nordic farm melodies, his genius shining from him, a heavenly light, as I danced on the dunes, joining my voice to the pure tone of his famous golden violin.

As for my role, this Carmen, I loved and hated her. She was passionate, beautiful, but more selfish than anyone that I had ever met, insufferable in foolishness. I hated how she squandered the love that she was lucky enough to get. And yet, when I became her on the stage, when I wore her skin, everything that confused me about her character suddenly made sense. The Gypsy took over. My flesh, my face, was simply the mask she wore, my voice the instrument she sang through. I loved her, all of her, her strengths, her flaws, as I pranced bare-toed on that swept wooden stage.

I never forgot that I owed this chance to my master. He trained, was still training, my developing voice, and more than that, he acted as my invisible manager, arranging my roles. I was supposed to play the smaller part of Carmen's friend who sings six bars in act three. It is a good role, for a beginner, one that a singer of my status should be glad for.

La Carlotta was supposed to sing the leading part (and never mind that she was twenty years too old for it – no one could tell from the stage. Her face was smooth beneath the make-up) but three days before the curtain went up, in the middle of a dress rehearsals, her voice suddenly vanished. She had just taken a sip from a carafe of water, fanning her tremendous, glistening bosom with her handkerchief and in the middle of telling a filthy joke to the dresser who was working hard to keep those fatty glories decently contained, her voice was extinguished, mid-sentence. Poof. It went out like a candle.

She could no longer sing. She could not even croak.

Of course, it was a disaster. Andre and Firmin ran around like headless hens, squawking about cancelling the show, lamenting all those refunds when Meg, dear little girl, stepped forward and lisped, 'Messieurs, messieurs, there is no need to fear! Christine Daaé can sing it.'

I have no idea how she knew. Perhaps she heard me rehearsing the lead role with my master, locked in my room.

They laughed at first, nervously. Firmin twirled the rim of his fine beaver hat, smudging the nap with his fat fingers and said, 'It's true that she can sing, she is a wonderful chorus girl, but she is so inexperienced and even a diva would be hard pressed to learn such a role with only three days' notice.' He spoke to the room, as though I couldn't hear him.

I stepped forward, feeling invisible eyes on the small of my back, pushing me into the light. 'I can sing it, sir. My teacher has taught me the whole score. Why, I could sing the role of toreador, if you wanted!'

And sing I did, before either manager could ask me to reveal the identity of my teacher. The Habanera poured, like wine, from my mouth.

That evening, after the curtain went down and the tumult died, applause echoing in my ears like the memory of triumph, I returned to my dressing room. I was expecting a letter from my master.

I was not disappointed. He sent a sealed note, along with a bouquet of flowers, roses, blood red. I could hear him singing, somewhere. He was well pleased with me, and in such moods this was how he often chose to show it; an erudite letter, a small, touching gift, and a childish folk song cheerfully sung through the light fixtures. In such moments, I loved him more than I ever thought it was possible to love anyone but my father.

I had just cracked the seal, splitting his signature lyre down the centre, when I was interrupted by a knock at the door. The singing stopped, his sweet voice cut out immediately, completely as a candle snuffed.

It was the boy, the young Comte. I remembered him well, and in that instant I was happy enough to see him, but I was not ready for visitors. I needed to think.

I said no to dining with him. He took it as 'yes'. I don't think that boy ever heard a word I said. In any case, as soon as he had gone I knew that with him in town I would not be free to take the time I needed to perfect my role and prepare for the next one. I made a fast decision then, a plan that I spoke aloud to the walls (I knew my master was near, though still silent. It seemed quite natural to speak into nothing and know that I was heard) and I wrote a note to the Comte to give to Madame Giry who would discover where he lived, and gathered my things. I felt terrible, you see, for being so rude. I should have known by then not to expect empathy from an audience member. The public knows nothing of post-performance exhaustion.

I had three days to rest and I knew that it would be best to spend them with my father. He had not left my mind since rehearsals began.

I would have to return by Saturday morning, the seam-stresses had done their best reducing La Carlotta's voluminous costume, but it still required a bit of fine-tuning before the weekend shows. Three days would be enough to get to Brittany and arrange a memorial mass, assuming I caught the midnight train to the coast, which I would if I hurried.

I packed in a flurry, filling a small valise with money-purse, my good copy of *Faust* (I left the other on the table, fouled by last-minute rewrites meant to accommodate Car-lotta's slightly deeper voice), and clothes. I brought the flowers and thought I'd packed the letter too, but I must have forgotten it. Oh well, I dismissed it, words are not milk. They keep perfectly well.

I fell asleep in my second-class carriage, my cloak drawn round me like a coverlet, my head propped on the window pane. When I woke, I saw the coast.

8.

The village hadn't altered much in the five years since the funeral. Father and I had lived with the Countess in her Paris home where he received the best care possible given his disease, not that it did him any good. Right before his death he asked her for two boons, both of which she granted. The first was that, after his body was waked and the flesh had grown cold, he be retuned here for burial. It was the sight of his greatest happiness, I was glad that she allowed him that.

He lies here now, in the churchyard, the buried coffin has long-since collapsed; the earth hummock has sunk in on itself like Little Meg's empty cheeks. But when I checked, on my way in to speak with the priest about the service, I saw the old-style Celtic cross I'd ordered. I stooped before it, touched the sharp incision that formed his name. Granite seems to hold its edge forever. I am glad that I won our argument. The white marble the Countess wanted would be worn already. Beautiful things never seem to last long exposed to elements on earth. I laid my flowers down, the roses my singing master gave me. They were startling on the grassy grave, too red, too passionate a gift for a father from his girl, but I thought that they were appropriate, too, in a way. A gift from one father to another. It was, for me, a means of joining both the spirits that I sang for.

The Countess had also granted the second boon that Father asked her. She'd adopted me as her daughter, though she hesitated at first, for longer than I then found proper. Now that I am grown I understand her hesitation much more fully than I did, although I had an inkling even then. The variety of love she felt for me must have made the action seem incestuous to her. It was easier for her to sign the paper once I made it clear to her, as kindly as I could, that though I loved her truly, I could not reciprocate in the manner she desired. She wept a little when I told her this, her clear cheeks became mottled as chicken skin: few north-toned beauties are lovely in sorrow. Still, she came through in the end, and we grew closer, until we were nearly like sisters.

As far as I know, she was never jealous of the love I received from other sources. Still, I never could get used to calling her 'Mother', and in truth she seemed so relieved at this omission that it seemed to make our relationship far more comfortable than it had been before.

I entered the ancient stone church through the side door, passing the netted pyramid of exhumed skulls that flanked the wall, dried bones waiting to be rehomed in the ossuary. This church was new before the battle of Hastings. The inside seemed very rough compared to the splendours being unveiled in Paris. I thought it unlikely that anyone would attempt to apply the new trend of 'refurbishment' in such a backwater, and I was very glad. In the city architects were knocking down the crude, blackened rood screens in even the smallest parish churches and replacing the rough, column-like saints with more modern replacements, statues like the ones draped all over the Opera House. Do not misunderstand me. I loved those wonderful odes to the delights of the flesh, but in their proper place. The spirit is a harder thing, more granite than marble, less lovely than we'd like to think, but more enduring than the earth.

The altar was a bare stone slab, covered over with clumsy bundles of foliage spread out like an offering. The priest, a spare old man in a plain brown robe (it looked like it was made of burlap), was reaching up with the plate and wooden chalice, stretching to place them back in the cabinet which held the sacred bread and wine. He shut the door, painted with a scene of the Last Supper in tempera, turned and smiled at me broadly, so that every blackened tooth showed.

'Why, if it isn't Miss ... Daaé?' He rushed forward, tottering, his thick white hair shining in the sunlight let in through clear windows.

'Why yes! You remember me!' I remembered his kindness to me, after the service, but that was years ago.

'Of course, my dear. It isn't often that piety and beauty meet, I note it when it does.' He patted my hand like an uncle, 'Besides, you sang so sweetly at the burial that I have never forgotten it.'

After such a greeting it was an easy joy to arrange the memorial service. He would sing it the next morning.

'No, no, my dear. My Lord in Rome would be loath to hear it, but I take no payment for masses given in mercy. Weddings either (I can get away with it, there are not many). I have to charge for funerals, unfortunately. We have them pretty frequently, and my Cardinal does check.' He laughed, escorting me down the aisle like a bride in reverse, 'If you are so moved, however, I will say that we have a lot of poor in the area. If you are determined to part with some pennies might I suggest giving them to Madame Guilfont? She is a widow, you know, with seven children. Her husband had an enormous appetite for life, and love – until he suddenly didn't. Here, I will give you her address.'

The only paper I had in my basket was the script for Faust. He scrawled on the back. I was happy to see that the cottage was very close to my hotel. I would call, on my way past. She would get more gold than coppers.

9.

I spent the night at the inn in relative comfort. I never used to be so inclined towards luxury, but my years with the Countess have softened me so much that the rustic little room with the peasant-style, rope-sprung mattress and clay washbasin (there was no mirror) seemed quaint, if not totally uncomfortable. The bed was stuffed with feathers and the linens were clean, so I enjoyed my sleep and rose with the dawn, to the sound of the stable boy's wood chopping and the rooster's loud crow.

I had a hand-sized looking glass in my valise and I set it on the highboy dresser. The little mirror leaned against the wall and showed me enough of myself to reassure me that my hair had not become too dishevelled as I slept. At a little after six-thirty, the maid knocked with the breakfast I requested: a hot roll and a steaming mug of coffee. She left the tray precariously balanced on the mattress. I knew that since I meant to have communion during the mass I should defer satisfying my stomach, but I was so anxious about maintaining my strength for my performances that I did not want to risk wrecking my singing by altering any more of my schedule than was necessary.

'Oh, Madame?' The girl was young for this work, eleven or twelve, dressed in a frock that began its life as a flour sack. Perhaps she was the daughter of my host. She was a thin little thing and could have used some feeding up.

'Yes?'

'There is a Gentleman here.' She blushed, quite prettily. 'A young and handsome one, with a nice little moustache. He arrived late last night and asked about you. He wanted to know if you were going to church. If so, he wanted to know when you would be leaving and he offered me a bar of chocolate and a five-franc note if I will tell him so.'

Raoul. The little Comte. Did he not read the letter I sent him? I fumed, internally, carefully maintaining a light-hearted mask. Of course he read the letter. That is how he knew where I was. But then, if he read it, why did he not take me at my word that I wanted to be alone? I answered myself: because when you speak he hears only what he wishes to. He has always been like this; it is a habit from childhood.

Think, Christine, think. You have to decide what to do. You know that he is petulant. You know that he is spoiled, and that his brother loves him dearly. His brother is your boss. If you rebuff his advances too harshly, this boy could ruin your career just as it is launching.

The girl was staring at me, her big brown eyes open wide, waiting for a response. Suddenly, one came. It made its way to my lips as though in answer to an unspoken prayer. I must feign pleasure, play the game with him until I could return to the city and ask advice from my master. The 'Opera Ghost', as the dancing girls call him, was wise (I thought) in the ways of the world. I said, 'Of course, dear. The Comte. I know him very well.'

I smiled at her, allowed my grin to widen as her body relaxed. 'Go wake him now. Tell him that the service begins at eight o'clock, and that if he should wish to walk me there I will be waiting by the front gate at a quarter to the hour.'

The girl took my coin in exchange for a country attempt at a curtsey and clattered out into the hall in her antique wooden shoes.

I paced the floor for fifteen minutes, thinking about everything that I knew. The Comte's elder brother ran the opera house and kept La Sorelli as his whore. She bedded him and, because of this, had the honour of being the prima ballerina in the company, in spite of her drinking, while toothless Little Meg (the better dancer) held a secondary role.

I am the best singer in the company. My master is train-ing me to be the best in the world. If I deny the boy, Raoul,

I will continue my training. He cannot affect the quality of my work. He can, however, affect whether anyone hears me singing. I shuddered at the thought of years spent wasting my talent on the most minor of roles. Oh, how I hate politics!

I had to force my hands to unclench and break from fists before my nails pierced my own thin flesh.

I knew that my master would help me as much as he could, but how much influence could he have in the larger, more visible world where money means power? If I could endure the day, return to Paris safely, without being pushed into making a formal commitment, I would learn the answer to that question. It might even prove to be a satisfactory reply. Until then, I must simply endure.

Raoul, why couldn't you be happy with friendship? I liked you well enough, when we were children. Why couldn't you leave it at that?

I had my father's rosary in a box at the bottom of my bag. The beads were carved from sandalwood and had a wonderful, calming smell that deepened as they drew warmth from my hands. I wound the necklace twice around my wrist and brought the onyx crucifix to my lips to draw strength from the hanging body of Our Lord. This was as close to traditional prayer as I ever seemed to get (my singing was much more like the thing itself, no matter the words) and the feel of it caused something deep inside my heart to relax.

I dressed in a hurry, regretfully eyeing my untouched breakfast as I used the bedpost to draw in my stays, tying the ribbons to the pole and leaning forward until my waist was reduced enough to constrict my breathing. This is one of the benefits of opera; when I perform I am allowed, and expected, to have a natural waist. Once I was presentable, I headed for the door.

Raoul was waiting for me at the gate, he must have hurried to meet me, although you'd never know it to look at him: not one hair was out of place, his hat was freshly brushed, his shoes were shined, even his moustache was perfectly trimmed. If I were an ordinary girl, with the usual goals – marriage, money, multiple babies – I should have found him quite charming. I admit, he was more than a little attractive, and although he acted much younger than he was (I am convinced that immaturity arises out of ease) we were of an age, ready for whatever love we were made for. It was, after all, springtime.

I had been annoyed by his presumption at coming to see me against my explicit wishes; I worried about his motives and wondered how I could possibly rebuff them without consequences, but now that he was actually here beside me he was utterly charming. He did not press his company on me, beyond the fact of his presence. He was content to walk beside me in silence, beneath the blooming fruit trees (such foul smells, such bright colours!) occasionally tapping me on the arm in the annoying, commanding way men have when they are setting the pace.

The path through the tree-filled churchyard was a field of emerald sewn with buttercups, the gravestones rose, white and black, like shadows and the only spectres were the heaped pile of skulls, a sprawling pyramid, propped against the rough stone wall.

We entered together, but Raoul did not break propriety by demanding to be seated beside me, taking his seat on the right with the few other men who came up from the village to breakfast on God. I sat with the women, elderly peasants (most wore white headscarves) and tried to pray in the conventional fashion while the priest sang the mass dedicated to the memory of my father. It was so good to know that there was at least one room full of people, at least, who would remember him in prayer. When he lifted his arms to raise the blessed Host, the loose brown sleeves sliding past his hairy elbows, he said my father's name as a part of the blessing and my spirit was filled with a beautiful calm; all my worries vanished.

I was lucky enough to have two Fathers, one in heaven watching over my spirit, one to care for my body on earth. Nothing could harm me, not even this over-eager young man. I was perfectly safe, protected, and would remain so.

When the time came, I approached the rail to take the Body on my tongue. The priest placed it in my mouth whispering, 'The body of Christ, broken for you'. Raoul and I had been seated in parallel rows. He had come up with me to the altar. As I chewed, swallowed, I happened to glance beside me. The boy was glaring at the priest, like a husband at a rival lover! There was so much hatred in his look, such pale rage directed at a kind old man who had touched me only in blessing, that I was filled with fear so great I nearly choked.

I swallowed as carefully as I could and rose, taking hold of the rail for balance – my hands gripping wood polished by centuries of prayers and entreaties. I made my way back to my seat.

After the service I stuck close to the priest, thanking him over and over again for the service he gave. He must have sensed some animosity from my 'friend' because when Raoul attempted to interpose his body between us, offering to escort me back to the hotel and then to the train station, the old man interjected that I might prefer to spend some time alone near the tomb of the Christian that I had come all this way to see.

I thanked him, agreeing, and Raoul took the hint, saying as he left, 'Well, I suppose that I will see you again in Paris. After all, you still owe me a dinner. I will pick you up tomorrow, after your rehearsal.'

I agreed to join him then, to give me freedom today. I was seething beneath my calm.

I spent several hours there, sitting in the grass with my father. The crimson petals of the roses I'd left were already wilting on the green. I returned to the hotel in the late-morning, to pack my bag and buy a sandwich. By the time the sun set again I was on the train, speeding towards Paris.

ERIK

7.

There is a vast, oceanic difference between ugliness and deformity. Ugliness is human, a distortion of what is commonly perceived as the natural. An ugly face gives no pleasure to the fishwife passing in the street, but neither does it disgust her. Deformity, especially of the face, causes repugnance to rise like vomit in the breast. It goes against that which we like to call the kindness of God. I have never known my face to give pleasure to the world; it is exceedingly difficult for me to imagine that it could. I am not used to thinking of myself as human. Perhaps if all the faces in Paris were marred by the pox I could walk about maskless. In such a situation, with everyone about me, from the fairest maid to the most destitute prostitute blinded or riddled with pustules I would find my status raised. I would wake to find myself no longer a monster, a mere ugly man, one among many.

Since this is so, it is understandable that I was slow to comprehend what was really developing between Christine and myself. I had never thought of myself as a possible object of love. I know what I am. After seven years with that carnival it would be impossible for me not to be aware of my place in nature. I honestly believed that I saw her as a student, at most a daughter. God knows she was happy enough to see me as a stand-in for the father she had lost.

Though 'see' is the wrong word. Before our sojourn underground she had only met me once in the flesh, and at that time I was wearing mask, wig, and gloves.

Sitting here, alone in darkness, looking back across the gulf that separates 'then' from 'now', I can watch the tragedy unfold clearly, without the blinding fog of confused passions which engulfed me at the time. Writing it down in this book that (I suspect) will be read only by myself enables me to examine our motives, as though through a mirror. I see the flaws that I was blind to, then. I see myself, a great ragged bird, displaying my courtship feathers.

When I started giving her lessons I was enamoured only with the potential that I saw in her voice, her potential for genius. Our lessons progressed for quite some time without interference or interruption from external or internal forces. It was a delicate balance. True, when we were meeting on the scaffolding high above the stage (the one sure place we had for privacy before she earned the privilege of a room of her own) I made the space as comfortable as I could for her, sweeping out the filth that Bouquet left behind while he lived (that was one body that they never found, as far as I know he is still hanging from that beam in the basement, above the corpses of the architects, unless the rope rotted, or his neck). The man was a pig and his sprinkled food wrappers had attracted many rats. How could she have focused on her work in such a place?

So yes, I decorated. Laid down carpet, a few pillows, I added some light. And yes, I gave her gifts when she did well, small motivational treasures when she began to be cast in singing roles. That tortoise shell comb, the music box, roses (in season), toys. I never questioned why I did it. It only seemed right.

And oh, how her face lit up when she found them! Oh, how she smiled, reading the letters I wrote in my unpleasant hand!

In retrospect, I can see how the problem began. If that boy had not thrust himself in our path, brought himself to my attention, brought my love to my attention by threatening its loss, we could have continued as we were, for years, happily dedicated to art, or should I say the great work of the spirit, without getting our filthy bodies involved. I would be the last person to choose to be bogged in the flesh. These mobile bags of rot ruin everything.

A beautiful dream, but it was not to happen. When Christine returned from her impromptu visit to the grave of her father she was agitated, red-cheeked, pacing her room in exactly the same manner that I paced my cage in the early years of my captivity.

I hid in my usual place, the crawlspace between her wall and the secondary rehearsal room; a space I designed for adequate passage. I spoke to her, throwing my voice in reply to her questions so that my answers seemed to spring from one or another of the gaslight fixtures. I had rigged them, by this time, to flare at the push of a button, for emphasis. I could see her through a crack I'd made in the wall, a fissure as thin as two sheets of good paper. She was pacing so quickly that her shadow made the light seem to shutter: the dark of her body, the bright white light. She was more beautiful than I had ever seen her. In rage, her voice was like warm, wet silk drawn against a frigid cheek.

'And then, when I specifically asked him to stay away,

what did he do? He showed up! At the very hotel where I was staying. He came with me to my father's grave!' She stopped long enough to twist her rosary through her fingers, wrapping the beads tightly enough to restrict her circulation. She continued, sotto voice, 'If all he wanted was an affair, I could do it. It would be a sin, but a lesser one than sacrificing my voice, my one contact with God.'

When she said that my bowels clenched, a sensation I ascribed at the time to a meal that I had improperly cooked.

She spoke again in a louder voice, pacing once more. Her small feet were wearing a thin path in the fine pile of my carpet. 'But it is so much worse than that. When I returned home, the Countess said that there was a letter waiting for me. I opened it, thinking perhaps that it was somehow from you. It was from him. He wants to marry me. He wants me to stop singing in public, like a good bride and "save your songs only for me". The selfish, spoiled pig! If it were anyone else on earth, I could say no and be done with it. But his brother owns the theatre, his brother Philippe who is keeping Annie as head dancer, even though she is a drunkard. In the end, the rich get everything. He will give the boy what he wants!'

The boy, she called him! As though she were older; she was little more than a girl herself.

I spoke to her then from the candle on her dresser, behind her left shoulder. I kept my voice as calm as I could manage, 'He cannot, would not, make you lose your place if you refused him. The Opera Ghost would threaten them, and would follow through on those threats. The stage would be slick with spilled blood.'

She stared into the flame until her eyes were sockets filled with gold, 'True, but no amount of threats could make them give me decent parts. And I would rather die than bow and spend my life as something less than I could have been.'

We were silent then. In that instant I knew that I loved. It felt like a death.

She broke the silence, looking up from the candle, her eyes meeting the nearly invisible gap in the pine-board wall, the place where I hid from her. She spoke, 'There is something else we can try. I know that you are there. I feel your eyes on me, wherever I go, wherever your voice seems to spring from. I feel your eyes on me, and they burn.'

She dropped her gaze, and it was a mercy.

'I also know that you are no ghost. You are a man. You love me for what I do, and you wish to protect me.'

I could not speak. How could I answer? I rested my masked forehead on a splintery lathe, my hands gripping each other. Though I had washed, the rotten stench of my body filled the small space where I hid like a dead rat wedged between floorboards.

She approached the wall, turned, rested her spine against the rough boards. Her voice was so soft. 'Please, please don't leave me. I did not mean to frighten you. I need your help.' Her hands pressed behind her, palm down on the wood, her small fingers curled. 'Tell me you're there.'

'Yes.' It was all that I could manage. I did not throw my voice. The sound was right behind her. Nothing but a half-inch of wood kept our corpses apart.

Her head drooped. I could see her hair, smell it, but I was blind to her expression. Her voice was so soft, a perfect instrument. 'If you are a man you must live somewhere. You have been a father to me. I could visit.'

Instantly a plan formed, it flared like a Lucifer stick. I could breathe again. My fingers unclenched. When my lungs were filled, I spoke to her, whispering, my near-lipless mouth mere inches from her perfect ears.

'Christine, listen to me. You must agree to marry him.'

She gasped, 'No!'

I continued over her protestations, 'I said agree, not "do". You will not have to go through with it. Agree to be his bride, accept his ring – if he is foolish enough to give it. But make the following conditions. First, that you will not be with him physically, you will not be alone with him, until the wedding has occurred.'

She turned her face to the crack, her dark lips smiling. I had never been so close to her before. When she spoke I could taste her sweet breath. 'How very proper! Keeping the lily white for the wedding. He will like that! It will appeal to his hypocrisy.'

I laughed, continued, 'Yes. I thought he might. But let me go on. Second, you must convince him to wait until the end of the season, say that you will not be able to break your contract. I expect that since his brother owns the theatre he will try to convince you otherwise, but hold firm in your resolve. At least convince him to allow you to sing the role of Marguerite at the debut of *Faust*. If he balks, say that you will marry him before the second show and that tuneless harpy La Carlotta will reprise the role from that point onward. Look into his eyes and tell him that your heart longs for one more moment on the stage, before you give it up forever and settle to your life in his shadow.'

Her left eye was seeking to penetrate the crack I hid behind. I could see her straining to see me and though I wore my mask I was glad that the light in her room prevented her from comprehending my darkness.

'On the night of the show you will sing even better than

usual (you and I will work very hard from tomorrow). You will have to work the whole script through. I will wait for the appropriate moment and at that time I will come and take you away. I cannot tell you when, exactly. In order for this to work your shock must seem real. I will keep you safe for a few weeks, long enough for the mystery to grow and the rumours to spread, but never fear the scandal will blow over and the time will pass in a flurry. We will have plenty of work to keep us busy. The boy is a problem, yes, and he has too much power. He is young, and impatient. But be assured that by the time you return to the surface and reclaim your throne he will have discovered another goddess to worship. I will see to it. It will be a gentle ending to the trouble he has caused.'

'I trust you, Master. I will do what you say. Immediately. But...' She took her well-formed bottom lip between her teeth and bit. Suddenly she was a child again, how my heart yearned to comfort her, 'how will you make me vanish? Where will we go?'

I answered very gently, 'It is better that you do not know that yet. You are a phenomenal operatic actress, Christine, but if this is to work it must be completely spontaneous. It must look like a real abduction. You must be frightened. Go now, daughter. Do your work and leave me to mine.'

I left before she could answer, following my hidden trails, winding my way through the bowels of the Opera House, until I arrived at my home.

8.

I built my subterranean home while the siege suffocated the city above my head and my Opera House stood empty, unfinished; the ruins of what never was. There are few things in this world more depressing than unfulfilled potential. Well, never mind. My building was completed, and if it is not *exactly* as I would wish it at least it stands, as perfect a creation as the world would allow to exist.

Christine would not be ruined on my watch. Her voice was very good and getting better all the time. Soon she would be ready to bring the final, the best, plan of my life to blazing completion. I was attracted to her genius, yes, but at first only because it was a complement to mine. She could sing and act like no other. She could take even the poorest of scores and imbue it with life – soon she would overtake the masters of her craft. When her voice reached the final level of purity possible for the human voice to attain she would need to have something to sing, a composition worthy of her skills.

If my face could never be presented to the world, my music would be. Christine would be my mask. The opera that I was writing for her would prove to be my opus and unlike the Palais Garnier this design would bear my name. At least, that was my hope.

You see, my time in the carnival, my sojourn in the pit of hellish human depravity, was not wasted. Frankly, I do not believe that *any* suffering is meaningless. Only cowards choose to do nothing with their pain. I could not write down the music I composed while trapped in that filthy cage. My hands were bound and I had no tools, but I could listen to the music of my blood, and the cheerful songs of the calliope (folk tunes, base trash, a few scraps of gold in the terrible faux-joyful dross), I could build on the strains that surrounded me from the cries of the monkeys to the love-whispers of the lovers who used the sight of freaks as a catalyst for oestrus.

I could memorise the notations that I wanted – and then I could perfect. After many years I had completed the mental equivalent of a thousand handwritten pages.

I had spent the last five years working steadily on the music, transferring the score from synapse to ink so that I had hundreds of pages of melodies, arias, fugues written and waiting to be arranged into story. All I lacked were words and plot. A focus for the tune. And now, thanks to Christine, it had finally appeared.

Of course it was about love; the bitter, desperate longing of the impossible unrequited, a love which spoils the moment it is tasted, the second the fruit hits the tongue. This was my 'Don Juan Triumphant'.

You see, I thought there was no hope of happiness for us. If I could not triumph over failure, I decided that I would triumph *in* failure. If my story could not be perfect, it would be a glorious ruin; the thing itself and no false trumpery. It would be better, anyway, than a false perfection, an ending tacked on to draw in the crowds. When Christine was here with me, perhaps even sitting beside me on the bench of my organ as I composed to her voice, I could tie the threads of song together and complete my final, greatest work.

The debut of *Faust* was two weeks away. She would sing this new *Carmen* seven more times and the last three performances would be very trying for her since she would also be rehearsing *Faust* at the same time, ready to bring her innocent Marguerite to grease-painted life. In the meantime we would intensify her training. I planned on working her voice for a full four hours a day.

It was such a pity that the critics could not recognise the brilliance of Bizet. The reviews of the opera were mixed, with glad exception given to Christine's performance. She was universally agreed to be a triumphant find for those two idiot managers.

I rarely pitied anyone, but my heart broke for Georges Bizet. The critics damned his unquestionably dazzling work with the faintest of praise, while at the same time reporting that the composer was very sick, possibly dying. It would be a terrible thing to leave the earth imagining that the world viewed you as a failure.

Ah, what did it matter? The music would live. The body would compost. Such was its nature.

I had much to do: an abduction to plan, bombs to wire, explosions to plot. I had to build a place to house the girl once I'd taken her (she needed to be comfortable). I might possibly have to dispose of a few extra bodies, but that was not so much of a problem. My chambers were vast, and mostly empty. Bouquet and the architects could stand some more company.

I settled on a space I'd excavated during the first construction of the building. A chamber, within calling distance of my own but, I thought, far enough to avoid temptation. It was originally intended as a Persian-style bathhouse for the star performers and wealthier patrons to relax in. There was originally going to be a cool, clear pool carved from a chunk of cream-coloured marble. It was never completed, and never finished once building resumed. The carved marble was there, a ten-metre oval, like a boat or a half-flattened egg. The walls were tiled with Indian porcelain squares depicting painted scenes from the Hindu holy books. There were countless gods, all doe-eyed, beautiful, caught in acts of creation, destruction, ecstatic copulation.

I transformed the pool to a sumptuous bed by lining the bottom with thick silk-napped carpets and satin pillows stuffed with dove-down. I lined the walls with enormous standing candelabra so that every surface shone. There were pillars in a circle round the room, but the light from their mounted brass sconces was less flattering than the softer light of candles, so I left them cold. I brought in books on music, countless scores, to keep her occupied while I was working alone in my chambers. On an impulse I went out in disguise, a cloak, my second-best hat (it had a very broad brim), my mask tied, secure, and purchased a selection of dolls and stuffed monkeys, for her to talk to. Everything, in short, that I had longed for in my own imprisonment. Yes, I thought looking around, she will be very happy here.

Once the room was completed it was time for our lesson. There was no pretence of singing candle flames this time. I remained on my side of the wall, the dark side, where the rot was, but she knew I was there and I spoke to her directly.

9.

One week before the debut of *Faust* a small but devastating fire broke out in the secondary rehearsal room. Management blamed one of the 'rats', the ballerinas in training. Christine's room was not badly damaged, her things were secure, but the lingering residue of smoke was poison for her throat and, since the young Comte had been continuously inter-rupting her private practice sessions with gifts, demands for her company, and invitations for dinner that proved manda-tory (despite his enthusiastic agreement to 'keep the lily white' by never appearing with her unchaperoned) the man-agement agreed to allow their star performer to select her own practice space, and keep it secret from the public. They were unaware of her supposed engagement.

According to Christine, Raoul was charmed by the idea of a secret engagement. Half his visits revolved around planning their elopement to London directly after her first performance.

Christine laughed with me before our lessons began in earnest, deriding the enthusiasm of her would-be lover, but I knew her well enough by now to know that half her laughter came from nerves. We met in our old space, the scaffold above the flies, the day after the fire. Fifteen precious minutes of our session were squandered, allowing the hysteria to pass then calming her with song.

I sat in my usual place, high in the rafters among the defunct pigeon nests. It had been months since we had been together here and while I had arranged her space, brought it back to its usual level of comfort, I had forgotten to sweep up the oak beams that formed my seat. Feathers and the fine fragments of eggshells fell when I moved.

I was not good at giving comfort, being so unused to receiving it myself, but I recognised that temper was the shadow of her gift: if she could not storm at her leisure she would be unable to sing aloud in calm. I did my best.

'La Carlotta's voice will never fully recover, she will "mark" her notes for the rest of her life. Luckily, her volume remains. Most of the audience will not know the difference. The management will.' I plucked a dung-clogged plume from my shoulder in one gloved hand, it fell to the stage much faster than a feather should. 'Six months of her caterwauling and by the time that you are ready to resurface the management will be ready to triple your fee.'

She smiled at that. Good. I was growing tired of her doldrums.

She said, 'It was cruel of you to sabotage her.'

'I merely replaced a damaged instrument with a better one, nothing more. She was not harmed, even in fame. Her name will carry her.' I hummed a few bars of *Le veau d'or*. 'Besides, it gave you your chance. That was worth any cost.'

She looked up at the celling. I was less careful about hiding now; she knew where I was; my skeletal outline was visible among the thicker shadows of the beams, but I was careful that an outline was all she ever saw. 'What did you use to take her voice from her?'

'A trifle. It was a salve that I learned about in Persia, concocted from a fruit named for the venom of the king of all serpents. You must only touch it while wearing gloves; its juice (which tastes like honey) will burn your bare skin.' I was not used to smiling in my mask. The motion brings the scarred skin of my cheeks in contact with the cheesecloth lining of my mask, lacerating the delicate tissue. 'Come, you have only two hours before dining with that fool of a fiancé.'

'Don't remind me. I worry that I will wreck all our plans by exploding at his stupidity and telling him exactly what I think about him. Luckily, when I speak he does not listen. He is too busy admiring the shape of my beautiful mouth.' I watched her clutch the fabric of her bodice, twisting the sapphire engagement ring that hung hidden there, as though it were a tick whose head was burrowing into her skin.

'Never mind Christine. It will only last a week longer. Then we will be together, in the spirit and the flesh, ready to begin our work in earnest.' Her face lit up at that, grinning up at me like the happy child she had been. I had to pierce my palms with my thumbnails to gain proper control of myself, 'Let us begin where we left off, with the tenth bar of *Oui, c'est toi que j'aime*. I will sing Faust. You almost had it last time, but you are singing in a manner that, while tonally pure, is far too carefree. Remember, Marguerite has been accused of murdering her child, she is about to be executed, and she knows that since her lover has sold his soul they will be eternally separated when she is taken up to heaven. You must imagine what that would be like for her, after so much suffering.'

Down on the scaffold, suspended between Heaven and the stage, I watched a girl of twenty become the perfect Marguerite. She assumed a haggard look that was somehow terribly poignant, ideal for the role. Her dark eyes seemed to web and fill with the tears of a bereft mother contemplating yet another loss. She opened her mouth.

'Ah, this is my beloved's voice! His call has revived my heart. Amidst your peals of laughter, Demons that surround me, I have recognised his voice. His hand, his gentle hand draws me! I am free. He has come! I hear him! I see him! Yes, here you are! I love you!' She reached up to me, her body yearning for me as passionately as her voice, 'My fetters, Death himself, no longer scares me! Now I am safe! Here you are! I rest on your heart!' Such sweetness, such cautious joy! Tremendous, impossible beauty emerging from the slight frame of a girl. I have never wept in life, I nearly wept for her then.

I replied to her, my chameleon voice assuming a tenor, projecting my true desire, disguised in song, 'Yes, here I am! I love you! Despite even the efforts of the jeering demon, I have found you! Now you are safe! Here I am! Come, rest on my heart!'

I reached out to her, as thought I could bridge the gap I had created, ten feet of empty air, with the power of my song.

RAOUL

7.

After my brief visit with Christine on the coast I acquiesced to her desire to spend her return journey to Paris alone in prayerful meditation for the soul of her father. Her reception of me when we met at the hotel was properly cool, or rather it would have been proper had we been in a town that boasted of more than one hotel and I had shown myself at her door, uninvited.

I ascribed her brief reticence to temporarily lost bearings; females are terribly unsettled by travel, female artists doubly so; this is why performance is dangerous for the breed. In the end she confirmed my assumptions of affection, laughing on our walk to the church, gently taking my arm. I felt secure in myself for the first time since reading that letter. I had no rival; there could be no competition attempting to uproot me from her heart. She was still the same little dancing girl I'd loved since childhood, still grateful for a recovered scarf.

I remembered the handwriting that had unsettled me so much, that fine paper marred with crude, childish slashes, as though the words had been composed by a petulant infant. The author was obviously unhinged. I have heard that some members of the audience can become so fanatically enamoured with the objects of their desire that they succumb to the delusional belief that the singer they have become entranced with returns their affection to the extent that all their singing on the stage is aimed at them alone. I laughed at myself, at my insane jealous frenzy, comfortable in my first-class coach, surrounded by plush leather. The brandy I sipped was the exact temperature of my skin. The half-full bottle that I poured it from gently sloshed with the motion of ten tonnes of steel thundering on rails. I spilled not a single drop.

All through the journey my pleasure grew. I embroidered my fantasies and planned the best way to bring them to fruition. Three hours from the city I called for the porter, asked the servant to provide me with a portable writing desk (all decent cabins are equipped with such materials), some stationery, a selection of pens, 'And do not underestimate the quality of paper, or ink. I want the finest that you have available and I am willing to pay for it. However, know that if you fail to satisfy me, I will claim the difference from your tip.'

The boy they'd sent to serve me was younger than I was. He still stank of the country. I'd wager that less than a year ago he was baling hay and milking cattle. If I had cared to examine him closely I would not have been surprised to discover chaff tangled in his tousled curls, clinging to the roots.

Still, he understood the language of coinage, bowed, and returned to me laden with the supplies I'd requested. They were passable. The writing desk was a little splintered at the corners, but that couldn't be helped. Fine things are difficult to keep on trains, and this one was mahogany, a wood which is lovely to look at but easily fractured. I tipped him a franc and set down to work.

I still have the letter I sent to her house. I've kept it with all the others, bound with black ribbon. She left it behind her, God knows why. She had room enough to carry it. I am convinced that she took a full third of the things that I bought her, and she used all of the luggage we had in the house.

The paper is middling, the linen content low, but the ink was fine and it has not deteriorated – though it has yellowed at the edges. Look.

My Darling Christine,

How I value our time together! Not every daughter is so dutiful to a parent long-since dead. I am so glad that you are. Such a fine trait will translate well into marriage.

I am certain that you think about it. Marriage. That you wait for it with joy. I am certain that, gifted as you are, you have long since grown tired of singing for your supper. You long to enter your own home where, like the child you once were (and remain in your pure heart), you will sing only for your husband, and your children, when they come.

Christine, I promise you that you will not have to wait long. In fact, I plan on rescuing you from your current circumstance as immediately as possible. The life you have been made to endure is not fit for a lady. You are a fine creature, meant to decorate a home and hearth, reflecting truly the glory of your husband. After I order the delivery of this letter I intend to visit an excellent jeweller I know of, near Notre Dame.

Never worry, my dear, I would not be so crass as to expect such a flimsy letter to serve as seal to our engagement. I expect that you will be waiting to speak to me. We will go out to dine with my brother and your soon-to-be-former managers. I will bring a gift to you, then.

Adieu, adieu, my love. Until we meet, I remain,

Your Raoul

I did not see her until the Friday performance. If she were my mistress I could have supported her happily and had her cease performing immediately, but if we held each other in sin I knew that I would never be able to hold her in marriage, and so she must continue, for a while longer, to show that voice (my voice) to the ignorant world.

She sang perfectly, as usual, and afterwards I met her outside of her rooms and offered her my ring, right there in the empty corridor, among all the tawdry props and folded screens of canvas. Of course, she accepted.

Her delicate lips curved in a smile both gentle and demure, 'But Raoul?' Her eyes met mine, no doubt questioning the propriety of a girl of her rank presuming the use of my first name.

I smiled down at her, until she met my eyes and I could reassure her, 'I am your husband, now, my dear. In all but law. Call me by my Christian name.'

She laughed a little, then. It was musical, of course, but then her breathing was musical, her pulse, 'No ... darling. I simply had a question to ask. Well, two favours really.'

I took her hand and held it. Her delicate fingers were hot through her glove. 'Ask, and you shall have it.'

I never expected her requests to break the bounds of propriety. Indeed, they did not. Both were eminently conventional.

'The first,' she said, lowering her face from mine so that her lush hair hid it, 'is that until we are wed, we never are allowed to be alone together. I would not wish either of us to fall into temptation. I do not want to smear your reputation, or mine.'

I laughed with mingled joy and pleasure, was this all she wanted? Well, it was easily granted. I wanted it, too. 'Yes, yes.' I told her. 'We will maintain our separate states, for now.'

But she was not finished. Once the issue of her modesty was settled, she withdrew her hand from mine and held me with her sparkling eyes. They were near-black, like garnets. 'The second request is rather more complex. You see, I have been contracted to finish the run of Carmen and then for the full run of Faust.'

'Yes, yes, I know dearest, but my brother owns the managers. He can free you from your duties.'

She did not seem as relieved by this as I had every right to expect. In fact she sighed! Sighed at me as though I were somehow being pig-headed and this was just what she expected!

'I know, but you see, it isn't for myself that I ask this. It is for your brother, and therefore for you. If I leave now, La Carlotta will have to take over if the theatre is not to cancel and take a great loss.' She twisted the ring I had just given her, a large, clear sapphire, around her thin finger, as though the stone constricted her, 'La Carlotta hasn't fully recovered her voice, or learned her music. She can sing a little, but when she attempts to hit the high notes she croaks. In two weeks, this will be different, she will have recovered and acclimated herself to her parts, but until then I should continue, for the sake of everyone else whose lives are bound to the completion of the show.'

I must admit, I was astonished by her generosity. Imagine, a girl delaying her own happiness for the sake of others whom she could hardly care for! It made me all the more sure that I had secured the right bride. I agreed immediately to defer our date. Two weeks could make but little difference. But then I was forced to ask, 'But how will you remain on stage, once news of our impending union reaches public ears? It would be irregular, not to mention immoral, for you to show yourself in public when you already belong in the bosom of your loving husband. It would be a slight against my rank.'

She smiled at that, her answer ready, 'I suppose that we could keep our "union" a secret until La Carlotta is ready to replace me? Think of it, our wedding will be a secret, a treasure, held between us two only.' She beamed up at me, her face radiating hope, 'It will make the final revelation so much sweeter at the climax.'

Of course I agreed, poor fool that I was. I had no way of knowing what the future would bring. When it came, I was blind, and helpless to stop it.

8.

The following weeks were incredibly difficult for me. It was torture to see her every night on stage (I had a box at every show, usually number 4. Madame Giry insisted that number 5 belonged to 'the Ghost'), but it was the right kind of torture, an agony most pleasurable. My mornings passed in the golden glow of expectation. Christine had rehearsals for most of the morning, dance first and then her private coaching. I would join her for a few hours every night, after the show.

She was silent with me then, in the restaurants. Tired, I expect, properly demure. She damped her gift, hid her nature, in order to set me shining among company. I had the supreme joy of knowing that she was so dedicated to my love. Beneath the table, shielded by the lace cloth, I took her warm hand. It bothered me that the finger was ringless, as it must be if our ruse were to be a success, but it comforted me to see the substantial lump it made in her bodice, where it hung on a chain, between her small breasts.

I nearly always kept my word about never being alone with her; her managers were usually with us, along with the Sorelli woman, and of course, my brother who eschewed convention by taking every opportunity to fondle her loose white bosom. They were hardly fit chaperones, but they sufficed to our purpose. Occasionally, while they were otherwise occupied, in the supposedly 'men's only' smoking room, or when they had retreated to their carriage, I attempted to sneak a chaste kiss or two of my own. Christine always, without exception, pressed her white-covered finger against my lips and gave me her cool cheek.

Such damping worked wonders with my soul and made the fires of my love blaze all the hotter.

She was right. There was a sweet and potent pleasure in knowing that she was mine, before God, and having the knowledge that all around us supposed us only to be courting.

My growing ardour was accompanied by its shadow, jealousy which grew like a weed, sharing soil with romance. I had nearly forgotten about the deranged letter I'd glimpsed in her chamber, but it killed me to know that her heart had a master other than myself. Her singing master. I know that every stage artist has one, someone learned, possibly a retired singer or another sort of musician, who can help the diva focus on her method and smooth the rough places in performance. I know that they are usually male.

Christine spoke of hers, occasionally, letting slip nothing personal. Everything she said revolved around work; the exercises that he was arranging for her, the training she must do, the constant repetition of a single long note. I was determined to meet him, hoping to find that the master was some frail, ugly old man, skilled in his work and otherwise utterly harmless. I needed to assure myself that I was secure in my love.

All that weekend, after our meals, after I had released my fiancée into the arms of the Countess, I lay in my bed brooding about this unseen visitor she had, telling myself over and over again that I had nothing to worry about, that no rival existed. It took me hours, every night, for sleep to cloud my head. I did not know, then, that fanaticism was overcompensation for doubt.

Once or twice, early in the fortnight of our separation, I had attempted to attend their lessons, just (I assure you) to ensure her comfort and to reassure her of my love.

I timed my visits very carefully, so that I arrived about a half an hour after they were scheduled to begin. I came each time with flowers, white roses, lilies (in honour of her dedication to purity), and the finest chocolates that I could purchase. Each attempt was frustrated. There was always someone around!

I would approach the hallway, pass by the room that the dancers sometimes rehearsed in, the ancient barre was reflected in the dust-covered mirrors so that when the girls danced I imagine that they resembled nothing so much as their own ghosts. I sped up my step when I heard voices, hers achingly sweet singing something in German, his pure and more masculine than I had imagined. It was impossible for me to believe that it spilled from the throat of a kindly old man! Blood pooled in my head at the sound of it. I gritted my teeth so hard they hurt and dug my nails into my own palms, crushing the stems of the flowers and staining my gloves with chlorophyll blood.

I would nearly reach the door before someone stopped me to ask what I was doing, and turn me away. On Monday it was grey-haired Mrs Giry on her rounds of security, the keys and other tools she carried clinked together on her fat, crepe-covered waist like a jailer's cuffs or the chains of a ghost. She spoke to me in her gruff, accented voice, 'Messier, you should not be here. I have orders.'

I tried to bribe my passage with a tip, but she had none of it. She even took my arm, if you can imagine the nerve, and escorted me from the door just as easily as if she had been a practised bouncer.

I tried again on Tuesday. This time, my passage was blocked by the box-woman's unsightly daughter, that Little Meg who dances like a sylph at a distance, but is so hideous up close. I tried to bribe her as well, offering a full twenty francs to win through the door. She would have none of it. It was all that I could do to maintain my calm. I held out my arm, the one not burdened by gifts, and attempted to push my way past her.

She stamped her little foot at me, crossed her arms across her chest, and threatened to scream for her mother! Remembering the unpleasant woman, I had no wish to rattle the cage of that jailbird. I left without trouble, presenting my gifts to my treasure after each evening show.

It is strange to consider what happened after Little Meg rebuffed me. When I made my third attempt, on Wednesday, I found that a small, unexplained fire had broken out in the room beside the one my love rehearsed in, the room of dancing ghosts. The flames were quickly quenched, but the smoke that lingered was enough to damage her voice should she remain to inhale it. When I made my inquiries as to where she was practising the managers said they did not know, and the other members of the company would not tell me. It felt, almost, as if there were some strange, dark conspiracy designed to keep us apart. I took the hint from fate and ceased seeking her before her performances.

Time would pass soon enough; I calmed myself by repeating that there were only nine days to go until our wedding. I had much to plan before her final show.

9.

The night came at last. Christine's final night on stage! After tonight she would no longer be forced to prostitute her splendid voice. After her triumphant curtsies, while the orchestra was still sawing away at the epilogue and the flowers were still flying to her feet, and as she gripped the hands of that fat Italian tenor who filled the role of leading man and bowed her thanks to the audience, I would rush out of the door and give the signal to my driver who would be waiting on the seat of the new white and gold carriage my brother had bought for me, led by a team of six perfect, cream-coloured geldings.

He would tip his hat at me, acknowledging my orders, and I would turn and rush, rude as I pleased, through the press and swell of finely dressed bodies thronging the stage. I would mount the boards between the shell-shaped floor lights, pulling myself up in one elegant motion, and claim my bride with a kiss on the cheek.

I had seen the costume that Marguerite was to wear for

her ascension to heaven; Mr Firmin had shown it to me. Or perhaps it was Andre. One of them had led me back beyond the props and clear-floored rehearsal spaces, into that land of gauze and satin hidden in the rear of the building, where shrouded women worked at weaving, embroidery, all the crafts their sex was created for (excepting procreation), stitching sinuous magic with their needles and thread.

I saw it hanging there, finished, the fabric still warm from the heat of her body as Christine's seamstress made adjustments for the final fitting. It was totally appropriate. A wedding dress of silk and tulle, a fit garment for the soul of the wronged woman to wear as she rose up to heaven (the flies were hidden with clouds made of sheep's wool) and became a heavenly bride. This would be the climax of the show, the garb I'd claim her in.

It was perfect, also, for my purposes – which were, admittedly, a little less than heavenly. Once I had joined her there, under the lights, I intended to sweep her up and bear her back with me, across the threshold, until we reached our new lives.

It was a beautiful dream.

Of course it did not happen. Instead of a happy groom with an ecstatic bride, I found myself alone, a man temporarily broken in body and spirit. Cracked by circumstance. Let me tell you how it came about. Let me tell you of the torment that followed, the hell that revealed the previous weeks, that I had thought torturous, for the heaven they had been.

Everything seemed to be going so well, until that last act. I sat with Philippe in the box with the managers. I couldn't see the harm in telling them what I had planned after the show. My brother clapped me across the shoulders in hearty congratulations, his fatty chins bunched beneath his neck as he smiled. There were congratulations all around, and everyone agreed that since La Carlotta had fully recovered there was no harm in letting my Christine out of her contract, in fact, they agreed that it was proper that she be terminated immediately, in order to focus her fine female energies on preparing for the wedding night and the conceptions that were surely soon to follow.

Firmin (or Andre) offered to send his twelve-year-old footman (dressed in full livery) to signal my driver for me, saving a trip: a proposal that I happily accepted. Sending the boy out when he did undoubtedly saved the child's life.

Everything had happened according to plan, until the last act. The orchestra was much better than I had ever heard it. The trumpeter who always hit his notes flat had mysteriously vanished, as had the cellist who could only screech his bow along the lower register. My brother said that they had filled the vacancies with musicians that the 'Opera Ghost' recommended in a letter. He said that he'd thought it was a joke, at first. 'Such handwriting! Like an untrained child's!' But the improvement in the orchestra was vast, so he was glad that the managers had pushed him to consider it. The new flies-man they'd hired after Bouquet went missing was much better, too, the scenery no longer clattered in its tracks as the scenes changed. Unlike his predecessor he worked in utter silence. There was no foul cursing from the wings to wreck the balance of a love scene or add unsought humour to a tragic death.

In short, everything that could go right had done so that evening.

My brother had eyes only for his darling Anna Sorelli who, I must admit, danced beautifully during the pastoral introduction. Her legs were long and muscular, her motions graceful. You would never guess that, off stage, she was a drunkard. The floor lights, and the golden light reflected by the crystals in the four large chandeliers above the third-class seats, brought out golden highlights in the hair she wore. For the moment it mattered not one whit that it had not grown from her scalp.

The pastoral ended, opening the opera. Philippe nudged me with his round elbow as she tripped off the stage, fluttering her plump fingers at him, an action that she no doubt felt subtle enough not to interfere with her role.

When Christine entered, dressed in her charming shepherdess' frock, all white lace and light-blue bodice, herding a few living, luckily docile sheep across the field, and started singing, the audience lost itself in gasps. She had been wonderful in Carmen, reducing most to tears. Now she was sublime. An angel dressed in the flesh of a mortal, her transcendent purity shining through that fragile skin so that she seemed to glow against the painted scenery.

Looking at her, I felt something cold and very hard fasten itself around my heart. I felt it tighten. She had not sung so well for her father. My eyes began to water, almost as though I were in pain. And here she was, finally, singing for me and me alone.

There was no doubt that she was a woman in need of a rescue. There is no doubt to my mind, even now, that I was the man meant to do it. But while she sang, God help me, I regretted it. For one instant, one instant only, I bought into the lie that she belonged on the stage.

I blame my failure on that.

The story progressed as usual. The fat man playing Faust pretended to be young again, he played petulant tricks on the neighbours, egged into action by his demonic assistant (who would prove to be the Master). I must say that, even then, the monster sounded familiar. But his face was covered with the dark cowl of a monk, his rail-thin body shrouded in folds of brown burlap, and I could not tell if I had ever seen him before. His voice was wonderful, better than Faust's. At the time I thought that the roles had been painfully miscast.

At the end of the play, as Christine was languishing in her plywood prison (her face and arms were the only things visible through the painted wooden bars of her cell), she sang something to Faust that, though I could not understand it, made my heart leap in my chest.

'Der Böse! Siehst du dort ihn sich erheben? Er stiert uns an! O schick' ihn fort! Was will der hier am heil'gen Ort?!'

She reached out through the bars, attempting to grasp hold of her Faust's fat hand, when suddenly there was a tremendous crash, and a lot of terrible, unmusical shrieking as several horrifying things happened at once.

The celling of the opera house has been painted with several murals in the fleshy, neo-classical style. These scenes of cavorting, bare-breasted goddesses are lit by several extremely beautiful chandeliers made of brass and fine, clear crystal. They hang above the audience. From the stage they are invisible. As my darling one reached out for the Italian there was the sound of an explosion, I thought that perhaps some oil pooled between the base of the lamp and the place where the screws met the plaster. In any case, it broke free and a full five tonnes of glass and metal tumbled into the cheap seats at the base of the orchestra, killing several people and spraying the carpet with dangerous shards, along with swift, consuming flames from the spilled puddles of oil that spread rapidly, hungry for the splintered wood of the stage.

Christine instinctively leapt back, thank God for that. The false wall of her prison fell forward, revealing that she was already wearing that fantastic white dress, her body wired for flight, her aborted ascension.

I saw the robed man, the painfully thin devil disguised as a monk, rush forward and catch her in his arms, dragging her away from the wreckage to hide in the shadows. My spirit thanked him for that. I thought he was saving her.

By this time the first shock had passed, and I found that my body could move again. I thrust myself from my seat, determined to reach her no matter what obstacles, no matter what vermin bled in my path. I would take her in my arms and carry her to safer earth. I fled from the box, my brother shouting behind me, begging me to find his Sorelli, as I ran down the long, temporarily empty Y-shaped stairway that led to the main entrance.

I pushed through the gilt doors, opening into a sea of screaming bodies. I was trampling down the aisles (I am afraid that I knocked down a child in my haste, a girl bleeding from the forehead) in my hurry to find the body of my love. I thought that Hell was here already.

I was not prepared for the tragedy to grow much worse.

Another series of explosions planted beneath the footlights rocked the stage so that it bent and fractured like a reed in a storm. The curved edge of the stage bent up, torn from its moorings. The lamps scattered everywhere. There was no doubt now that this was sabotage. I know the sound of dynamite; I was fond of such explosions as a child.

As the dust began to settle and the bodies which had blocked my progress had been either blasted to bits or pulled to safety in the floodlit hallway, I felt a hand on my elbow. It was my brother. His face was shriven in dust, crossed like it is on Ash Wednesday. He was weeping freely, though whether they were tears of grief or a reaction to the thick clouds of oily black smoke, I could not then tell. My ears were ringing so loudly that he had to shout to be heard. (I found out later that my left ear was bleeding. It never fully recovered hearing.) We pressed forward together, moving more carefully. He was more cautious than I was, avoiding torn limbs where he could. I trampled over them. I knew, in my heart, I was seeking a corpse.

In the end I found one. Philippe made his hands into stirrups, as he had in my childhood, after buying me my first horse. I mounted the stage and nearly collided with the body of the man who had been meant to play Mephistopheles. He was hanging from a rafter, suspended by the throat and revolving slowly, back and forth. In the thick dust, the smoke from the fires that the ushers were already struggling to extinguish, I could just make out his features.

He was too thickly built to be the man who had taken my treasure. That devil had a face that, the few times his cowl fell back and showed it, was shiny, as smooth as an egg. This man's features, though bloated, were prominent, cragged with age.

The truth was too much for me, shock had caught me up. My darling had been stolen and there was nothing, now, that I could do. I fell to the floor in a faint. By the time I revived the worst was over. I was reclining in the manager's office, on a fine leather couch. My mouth still tasted of smoke, but someone had been kind enough to bathe my face in water and wipe the blood from my hands with a soft, cool cloth. The managers told me that the bodies had been cleared, the survivors paid off and tended, the fire extinguished at long last.

The damage was extensive; it would take months to repair before they could open for business again, and they would have to find dancers and singers enough to make up half their cast. The dancing girls who lived were already whispering about the Opera Ghost. It was all they could do to pay off the journalists to minimalise the event in the papers.

It was very lucky for them, Mr Firmin assured me, pouring a generous measure of brandy into a glass, that Little Meg had twisted her ankle at rehearsal and so missed the show. 'It's very strange, isn't it,' he said, 'how sometimes God brings fortune out of tragedy?'

He swallowed the slug of brownish liquor, looking with sudden shame at my brother. 'I am, of course, so sorry for you both.'

La Sorelli had not made it. Her legs were blown to shrapnel. Mr Firmin told me later that the firemen had come upon us both up there on the stage, amid all the wreckage. I was unconscious at the feet of the hanged man. My brother was seated beside me, wailing like a wounded animal, Anna's ruined head in his lap.

We never did find the body of Christine. There was one headless woman in white that they said must be her, but I had seen the costume she was wearing and this was not it. This was some other unfortunate, shrouded in a shift made to mimic the angelic costume my darling wore. She was taken, I was convinced of it. They did not listen, did not believe me. They took my conviction for grief and urged me to rest for a week or two before returning with my brother to work.

I took the drink they offered me and swallowed without

tasting what it was that I poured down my much-abused throat. Half-deaf, my larynx scorched with smoke inhalation, I was weakened but not beaten.

Christine was alive, I knew it. She had only been stolen.

I comforted myself with the knowledge that stolen property could be taken back, returned to the person who truly owned it. I would have to hurry my recovery if I did not wish to discover her ruined. Who knew how long a monster could refrain from fulfilling the desires of the flesh? I knew that once white satin was fouled it could never be pure again. How terrible it would be to recover her, only to find that I had lost her in the eyes of the world!

It was lucky indeed that Little Meg had injured herself. It meant that I knew both where to begin my search and which questions to ask to pursue my course. Her absence, and her mother's, blocking me at every turn could not be mere coincidence. Knowing that was half the battle.

My brother was too lost in grief (it looked surprisingly genuine) to offer any assistance. I would have to ask Monsieur Firman for her address. Then I would be totally on my own. I must hurry my search.

CHRISTINE

10.

I knew that something was coming. My master had told me enough about what he planned so that when it happened, whatever it was, I would not be too terrified to move. I knew my master well enough by then to understand that his genuine love of music, when combined with his deep sensitivity to (and need for) drama, made it unlikely that his plan would take effect at any time before the climax of the show. In any case, I was glad that I had thoroughly practised the score and memorised the libretti all the way through.

Sitting at my borrowed dressing table my face was wan in the mirror. The managers had extracted La Carlotta from her room, prying her away like a crab from her shell, under staunch threat of termination, as she had not yet fully healed and so could not use the facilities. I had not been sleeping well these last few weeks. A result, I suspected, of the stresses of hard work, enduring the company of the young Comte, and (I might as well admit it) pure, unadulterated excitement at the adventure to come. I felt like the thing that I was faking, I felt like a bride preparing for a groom.

In a way I suppose that was exactly what I was doing. Getting ready for my marriage to my art. And yes, I was excited to finally have the chance to get to know my instructor. The hints that he had let slip about his past were few and tantalising. I had to know who he was.

At this time, I was still young enough to fool myself about his nature. You see, I remembered his strange appearance at our single meeting in the flesh – that odd way he held his body, as though his joints were as stiff as a corpse's. I remembered the strange, expressionless mask he wore, and the terrible odour that crept from the wall where he hid while we were speaking in my dressing chambers. But I thought that perhaps he was just a shy eccentric, like my father was. Certainly I knew I was a daughter to him.

I mistook my unspeakable attraction for filial love.

This room was nicer than my own, the mirror was framed, the light was better, the furniture was plush and covered with Carlotta's fine furs. It had better heating, too. A newer brazier.

Sighing over the face I saw, the pale flesh, the bones of my skull shining through the exhausted skin, I applied powder, kohl, brought life to my cheeks with two streaks of rouge that I carefully blended with the tip of my finger. I dabbed a drop of paint, like blood, to my lips to counterfeit that healthy maidenhead glow.

I thought about Raoul.

The young fool was capable of so much unthinking destruction. He thought he wanted me to be his life's companion while at the same time he was plotting to utterly, blithely destroy everything that was of any value about myself. He mistook my form for function, seeming for being. I sighed, if only I had been born ugly.

Wasn't there a saint for that? Father told me. Saint Uncumber, patron saint of escaping unwanted marriages and bearded ladies. She was born the beautiful daughter of a Celtic chieftain who converted to Christianity early and longed to join a convent and dedicate herself to God. Unfortunately, her father had other plans for her. She was to serve as a pawn in a political coup, as the bride of a pagan warlord who had become enamoured with her radiant skin.

In despair, she had gone into the church to pray for release from this bondage. She asked her God to make her ugly. And he did. According to the stories, she sprouted a glorious beard, long and lush, bright ginger.

Her warlord would-be lover no longer wanted her, and her father was so ashamed of the monster he had spawned, that she earned the right to enter the convent. She packed up, shedding ginger beard-hairs all along the road. By the time she crossed the threshold, took her vows, she was as beautiful as ever – a fitting bride for Christ.

I smile a little at that; imagine, a woman rescued by ugliness! It was almost too much.

I was in a trap, my beauty was the least valuable part of myself and yet without it I could not appear on the stage. Why is it, I wondered, that women have to be everything; beautiful, talented, cleverer than everyone and all three at once to attain their ambitions while men could do what they wished so long as, of those traits, they had at least one? If Piangi had been born a woman he would have spent his life in Tivoli selling fish.

I sealed the jar of rouge, placed it back in the drawer with all the others. My lips tasted of rendered pig fat and grounded carnelian. I put my thoughts of saints away, reminding myself that I was perfectly safe. I was to be rescued.

I thought about the white dress with the hidden harness

that I was supposed to wear at the climax of the fifth act. It would be so wonderful if somehow my master could make the seeming match the being and enable me to raise my arms and fly, up through the painted celling, up to where the angels were. I smiled at the thought, dismissing it.

I straightened my maid's costume. It was nearly time to begin.

The curtain went up, on time for once, and not snagging on anything. I watched from the wings as Mephistopheles appeared and made his bargain with Faust. I thought, at first, that there was something wrong with Monsieur Jordan, the actor who was originally meant to play the monk-mocking devil – his body was much thinner than it should have been, but the voice was the same rich baritone that I had heard in rehearsals this morning. I was about to dismiss it as a trick of the light, but then the man in the cassock turned toward where I was standing and I saw the wax surface of the mask shining in the hot lights.

Seeing him there I felt an undeniable thrill, a sharp, clear mixture of pleasure and agony running from my knees to my heart.

A part of me worried about the mask he wore. It would not be good for him if the heat of the spotlights started melting his wax features. He nodded to me once and then continued singing.

I entered when my cue came, ignoring the pleas of my would-be lover and trilling, 'No thank you, sir: I am neither a lady, nor lovely, and I really have no need for a supporting arm!'

The opera unfolded as it would, skipping from plot point to plot point, buoyed by song. I was brought to the notice of the powerful Faust, and allowed myself to be won with fruit and jewels. Then, I had the pleasure of singing on stage with my master. When Piangi, as Faust, gave me a ring, swearing me to him, I sang to him, 'These jewels do not belong to me! Please, suffer me to remove them!'

My master, the Devil, replied softly, thus, 'Who would not be delighted to exchange wedding rings with you?'

And so I was seduced, and bore a child by him. I was exiled from my family, held distant from my love, felt incredible pain and expressed it (like a pustule) singing.

I was right. He waited till the end to bring down the curtain. I was in the jail, costumed in white, secured in the harness, when the first explosion rocked the stage and the chandelier crashed down and crushed the first four rows of people. I was more frightened than I had ever been (little knowing what worse there was to come), half choked by smoke and plaster dust.

I leapt backwards from the wreckage when the plywood wall that formed my jail collapsed around me. I might have been screaming, certainly I was deafened by the racket of chorus girls beating each other about the head to escape from the tumult. Suddenly my master appeared from the midst of the fire like the devil he was playing. He took hold of my waist, and I was so relieved to see him that I buried my face in his cassock, dismissing the foul smell that rose from the fibres as a product of the burning.

There was a lever behind me that I was supposed to flip when the time came for my ascension. It was a pulley connecting my harness to a counterbalancing weight high up in the rafters. He held me up, flipped the switch, and up we went. It was weighted for my body and although he was very thin, the weight was more than doubled. He must have added something to it. As we rose to the rafters I thought

I saw another body falling, like a shadow, to the stage.

I found out later that it was Monsieur Jordan. Hung by his neck and then tied to the counterweight.

We landed on the scaffold where I'd had so many lessons at nearly the same moment that the other bombs detonated, casting the stage into splinters and slaughtering more innocents than I care to consider. The force of the explosion threw me to the floor and while I was struggling to stand I saw my master, lithe as a cat, his mask gleaming and expressionless, tossing a white-and-red bundle over the rail. A few seconds later it landed with a thump that I heard, in my mind if nowhere else, as the sound of meat chopped by a cleaver.

Before the fire was extinguished, before I had fully got my bearings, he had taken my hand and led me down, down through a series of ladders and secret corridors, to his dark kingdom in the massive, sprawling basement.

11.

Seen from the street, the Palais Garnier is absolutely massive. It stands on twelve thousand metres of land and rises, a marble mountain crowned with copper, a full five storeys tall. And yet this is nothing compared to the caverns which sprawl beneath the building, terrible tunnels containing chambers; some are black, muddy pits, others immaculately furnished. I never thought that such flawless beauty as in the room that he gave me could exist side by side with a mud-floored cave that reeked of the char-pit. And yet it did.

My mind was still reeling from the chaos up above, our rushed flight. It was as though I had become drunk on so much sudden fire and death. My master led me through the labyrinth, his hand gripping mine, alternately singing and laughing loudly enough to keep my eyes focused on him. The space back-stage was totally empty; the rehearsal rooms we passed looked utterly abandoned, as though they were haunted. Every living body save for ours was occupied with the rescue going on in front. I could not leave a thread behind me, or a trail of breadcrumbs to mark my passage. His voice sank into my brain, a hook to draw me forward, saving me from committing the sin of looking backwards, longing for the light.

Once, he slid aside a panel in the wall behind the manager's office (I had mistaken it for a slab of solid marble) revealing a secret passage and a narrow flight of stairs fashioned from the same substance as the enormous Y shaped staircase in the front foyer. I thought, as the doorway shut, that this building was, in a strange way, much like my mind; a splendid surface containing strange depths, hidden even from the people who inhabit it.

I remember my father telling me something similar about music. That the audience cannot possibly comprehend the full extent of the score, for the most part they listen to the melody, but the timpani beats away anyway, underneath it, setting tone, the vital pulse, and even without understanding what is happening around them, they feel its effect.

I have no idea how long we ran round those winding corridors. I know, now, that there are many ways much more direct that the path we took. Apparently part of my master's plan to 'keep me safe' meant keeping me with him, even if I ceased to wish his company.

I know it sounds foolish to say so, but it took me a surprisingly long time to understand that the explosions, all that needless violence and death, were part of his plan for effecting my rescue. I assumed that he would merely steal me after my assumption, possibly by bribing the new flie-master whose job it was to catch me as I rose. I knew, very well, that he favoured drama. I blame my dismissal of his motives on combined trauma and shock.

Certainly, by the time we emerged into my rooms (it would be some time before I saw his) leaving behind the unfinished well and the filth-floored room littered with stinking, reddish skeletons, I was utterly exhausted. Too spent to see that the walls were lined with images of Hindu idols engaged in acts of obscene play, though I did notice the enormous marble bed, like a giant egg, all padded with silk, the music stand, and all of those uncomfortably childish toys he'd brought to scatter round me.

My master bowed me through the doorway into that rich golden light, guiding me by hand to settle on the sump-tuous bed amidst the cushions and the silk-embroidered sheets. I was suddenly very aware of the dress that I wore. The unspoken context.

He stood before me and I saw him whole for the first time since the night that we met. Every surface of his body was covered by cassock, gloves, his glistening mask.

When he spoke, his voice was smiling, as it should be considering how very well his plans went, 'Well, my dear, here you are. All safe and settled.' He retreated to a tall dresser in the corner, returning with a tray, a bottle, a small, golden glass. 'I need to work; I must clear our back trail, and you must by now be utterly exhausted.'

'Yes,' I said, it was true, 'but I am too excited to sleep.'

'Ah, but you must, if you wish to preserve your voice for our training.' His tone maintained its cheerfulness. He was utterly jocular. 'And I intend for us to use the time we have before your marvellous resurrection very well indeed.'

He poured something red and very thick from the carafe. It smelled delicious.

'In the service of that noble goal, I have concocted something good to help you sleep.' He handed me the cup.

I felt the true weight of gold, pure, unadulterated. It was heavy in my hand.

There was no question. I drank it. The smell was as good as the taste – like liquefied roses.

I was overtaken with dizziness. My master gently caught my head in his hand (he caught the precious cup in his other) and guided me to the pile of pillows.

My last memory, before sleep overtook me, was the feel of his leather-gloved fingers trailing across my forehead in a motion that was tentative and shy.

'Sleep well, my angel. You are safe and secure.'

And in that instant, I fell from the world.

12.

I have no way of knowing how long I slept. I know that whatever drug he gave me was very gentle; my head did not ache, my thoughts were clear when I woke. I slept very deeply, and my rest was sweeter than it had been since I was a child. I was ravenous, of course, though that told me nothing. I had sung for four hours before my rescue, and singing is hungry work indeed. I need a good meal after every performance. With such an appetite it is no wonder that older divas are often enormous!

I lay there, perfectly still, for a few moments. My eyes were closed, but the light glowed through my lids. I had either not been sleeping long (something I doubted) or the candles had long since guttered themselves out and been replaced, the new ones lit.

'Good morning, Christine.'

My master's voice surprised me, coming so suddenly. Of course, I had no reason to believe that I was lying here alone. I sat up, opened my eyes.

'Morning?' I was taken by a sudden urge to yawn, and did so, blushing at my unavoidable rudeness.

He laughed. It was beautiful to hear, though eerie, emerging as it did from the closed, painted lips of the mask.

'Morning indeed, but only just. You slept the whole night through, as I knew you would.' He was wearing a very fine morning suit: a dove-grey vest, and an improbable top hat. He drew a gold watch from his pocket, opened the lid to examine the face of the clock. 'In half an hour the early birds who twitter up above us will be having their lunch.'

The watch vanished, 'You will be enjoying your breakfast.'

I motioned to rise and he waved me backwards, playfully saluting me with his hat, 'No, no, my lady. Remain where you lie. The dining room will come to you. I expect that you are more than ready for a good meal. After your brunch, we will set down to work.'

I smiled at the suggestion, glad to have something to focus on besides horror and death. 'And what will we be working on, Master?'

'My gift to you.' He turned to leave, paused, and faced me again so that he could look at me. I saw his yellow eyes glowing through the holes in his mask. 'I think that from now on, you had better call me Erik.'

I thought of this while he was gone, fetching my meal.

It was, in a strange and vital way, the most that he had ever said to me about himself. His hints of the carnival, his time with the Shah, could have happened to anyone. They might have come from a book. There is something deeply intimate about a name. Giving it grants power, implies submission. I thought of the way that men can be so free with the name of a woman while she must show respect by using his title. This gift struck an odd balance.

But this man was and still remained my master, far advanced in art. Could I therefore think of him as a human, as my equal?

I tried the taste of his name on my tongue. 'Erik.' It seems that I could. I so looked forward to our work.

The meal he'd made must have been ready, or nearly, by the time that I woke. He was only gone for a few minutes. He returned, wheeling a gurney that must have begun its life in one of the city's better hotels; a construct of immaculate mahogany and brass, well-polished and covered with a gleaming silver warming tray, a selection of fine flatware, a champagne bottle, and a bud-vase bearing a single blood-red rose.

Erik left for a moment, and immediately returned with two cushioned folding chairs which he placed on either side of the gurney, so that it became, in an instant, a small table.

It was not strictly necessary for him to help me from bed to chair, but the gesture was kindly meant and I thanked him for it. He sat me before the single china place setting, taking his place across the table, in a position to serve.

It was deeply uncomfortable, for a girl of my upbringing, to be served before a gentleman, much less eat a good meal while he had nothing. When I asked him if he would do me the honour of partaking with me, he shook his head.

'No, my dear. Forgive me. I have eaten already.' He lifted the lid of the steam tray, revealing a plate of warm pastries, fruit compote, thin slices of ham. 'Besides, it is incredibly difficult to force food through a mask. Your plate, please.'

I handed it to him, watched as he loaded it with half the contents of the table. Obviously, he'd planned on me consuming seconds.

I took it from him, full. I said, 'You could always take it off, Erik.'

He shook his head, and when he spoke his voice was low and sorrowful. 'It is unspeakably sweet, Christine, to hear my name from your lips. While you reside with me you may wander wherever you wish, trusting your reason. My home is your home, my life is yours also. You may ask me anything you think of, with one exception. You may never seek to look beneath my mask, and since occasionally I must remove it, you must always announce your presence to me when you enter a room, so that you never surprise me without it.'

I laid down my fork, reached across the table to touch his gloved hand. The smell in my nostrils was the scent of the rose.

'Are you so terrible, then, that I would hate you?'

Erik withdrew as though burnt.

He rose, turned from me, shaking. We were silent for a moment, but when he spoke his voice was as usual, perfectly controlled. 'Will you do what I ask of you, Christine, my angel?'

What could I tell him but 'Yes'?

He looked at me again, straightened a nearly invisible crease in his jacket. 'Good.'

His hat was resting on the music stand, beside a tiny silver bell. He placed it on his head. 'Finish your meal, child. I must go prepare for our lesson. I will return for you in an hour. The washing room is behind that curtain, there is fresh water; the wardrobe is full of new clothes. If you find yourself in need of occupation while you wait there are books on the shelf in the corner. Until then, Christine.'

I smiled at him, baffled by his sudden shifts in mood and deeply sorry for the pain I caused, although I in no way understood it. 'Goodbye, Erik. I will see you in an hour.'

He left and I engaged myself with the remainder of my breakfast, stuffing myself with bacon and the stories in a book. *The Arabian Nights* were beautiful in French.

When he returned we set hard to work. He was right about the gift that he had made me. It was beautiful, and a challenge for my voice. The study time required would be enormous.

ERIK

10.

I could not relax or enjoy my triumph until I had secured the secret of our passage. Once Christine was safely sleeping (I stood above her for a while, guarding her slumber like the angel she thought me) I extinguished the candles and left her to rest, nestling down in the covers like a child. I had to resist the urge to do more than stroke her smooth white forehead, reminding myself of the obscenity it would be to break her trust, even by performing so simple an action as stroking her hair while she was helpless, unaware. I must say that I was tempted. Christine was the first person that had ever touched me and not been visibly wracked by repugnance.

I took a much less protracted route to the secret stairway that led down to my lair, arriving in a fraction of the time that it took me to lead the girl here. I did not mind showing her the skeletons in my little earthen closet, no bones, dry or moist, could rise to harm her, but the more direct route contains a few fine traps of my own immaculate design that it would be difficult to lead a frightened woman through. This time, I was navigating alone.

When I reached the top of the stairs I uncovered the supplies I'd stocked earlier; the boards and bag of plaster. It would not do to erect a permanent barrier, I would have to leave here sometime, to go about my opera work, and while I had other exits they opened out on to the street and would not serve for every purpose. Instead, I laid the lathes across the entrance in such a way that they looked solidly mounted, but were really secured by a few flathead nails. Then I filled the gaps between the boards with quick-drying plaster, so that if the door were opened it would seem to lead nowhere but a solid wall.

That finished, the corridor hidden, the night well advanced, I returned to my rooms and changed into my travelling garments. It was a bittersweet moment for me, reducing myself to my terrible nakedness in a room without mirrors, knowing that if I were not to ruin everything that I had built and planned for I could never afford to be careless.

But then, neither would I ever be alone. The cost was worth it.

And no, I did not stop a single moment and consider the wreckage that I had made above in the theatre. I designed it, after all. It was mine to do with what I wished. And, in any case, none of the damage was irreparable. The six months it would take to bring the stage back up to scratch would simply provide time for Christine to continue her training, and that idiot Comte of hers to give up his griev-ing and start sniffing for a bride under other, more appropriate circumstances.

Fully dressed, mask and wig secured, I pulled on my gloves and sought the mirror I kept in the closet.

Mirrors! I loathe them like vermin, but it was necessary to keep one stored somewhere in order to gauge the effect of my disguises. My suit, cut in the style of the latest fashions (I sewed it myself, adding a few special features) fitted me well and lay against my body in clean, pinstriped lines. Pleased, I selected, tonight, the wide-brimmed fedora I'd bought from the mad but immaculately skilled haberdasher who operated in a shop near the Louvre. It is amazing how lifelike a well-made mask can look, when cast in deep shadow by the brim of a hat.

Pleased, I picked up my valise and made my way to the fine night-market that operates near the Seine. The stands stank of foul water, but the bins were filled with many grand treasures. There was nothing here that hadn't been stolen, but the markdown was good, as was the quality, and the stall tenders made it their business to ask very few questions of the people perusing their wares.

I found a stall selling dresses and selected a few fine styles in a variety of colours. Christine could not wear that wedding dress forever, no matter how fetching she looked in it. The designs I chose were, admittedly, a little young for her. But then, I told myself, she is young, and she thinks of herself as my daughter. These frilled things would be totally appropriate to the role, and since she was slight, they would probably fit her.

Next, I procured a selection of fine foods; flesh, patisserie, fruit, a few exquisite truffles, a few fresh vegetables. I ensured that they were double wrapped in wax paper before placing them in the bag with the new dresses. I would not wish to stain the fabric.

Finally, I purchased a small silver bell, for the girl to carry with her to ring should she encounter any trouble, and three sheaves of barred composition paper. My current stock was running low, the foot pedals of my organ were surrounded by crumpled wads of paper and the music stand was weighed down with finished notes.

I spoke to no one on my travels. I do not make a habit of haggling with vendors, and with my wealth I have no need to. Pleased with myself, heavily laden, I returned to my subterranean home by another, longer road. Thieves were much more likely to pursue me once I'd stocked myself with goods that I'd bought from them mere moments before. Quick turnaround meant that they earned much more of a profit if they could keep my gold, recoup their material and sell it again in their store.

In my time trading here, I had only been attacked once, and I thrashed both of my attackers quite soundly, beating them about the skull with the knob of my stick. I would have slaughtered my foes, thrown their corpses into the river to be pecked at by gulls, but I knew that if I had done so I would never have been allowed back into the market. I liked to trade there, so I endured the mild dissatisfaction of allowing them to live. Manners, after all, might vary by context but they should never be ignored.

Tonight I had no problems. I returned in time to check on Christine, she was still sleeping, of course. The dose I'd prepared for her was strong enough to grant her eighteen hours' worth of the slumber of the angels. God knew she needed it, after the last several weeks. Already the natural glow in her cheeks was being restored. Her breath came sweet and with gentle regularity, like the pulse under music. I left her after I placed her new clothes in the wardrobe, before her beauty made me weak.

I would sleep myself, now, for a few hours at least. When she woke she would be very hungry, possibly disoriented. I must be ready with a meal for her, and at least a few kind words, before expecting her to settle down to work.

11.

When Christine had sufficiently recovered we settled into our work, using my own part-finished music instead of the usual canonical scores. In some ways our work continued much as it had before. My student was as dedicated as ever and her long sleep had done wonders for her voice; she sang my score with a richness of tone, that was as clear and weighty as leaded crystal, but it was strange to have her stand so close to me as I pushed the pedals and manipulated the keys of my small chamber organ.

I was dissatisfied with the sound that my instrument produced; it was quite in the shadow of my student's miraculous voice, but I could do nothing about it. It was difficult enough for me to shift this five-hundred kilo cabinet down into this cavern, even with aid of the pulley system I designed. When I composed the songs I heard every instrument in the full orchestral score, including the wonderful sixty-four pipe organ built into the walls of the theatre above. Compared to that, this small cabinet was a bugle, good for granting the listener an idea of the sound without the full measure of power. I must be satisfied that Christine consented to assist me in my composition and try my hardest to wait to experience the full flower of my music when she returned to the surface world, bringing it with her into the light.

If I could never stand to live in the world again; if I nconsigned myself to shadows like the grave, at least this part of me (by far the better part) would meet with resurrection. I smiled beneath my mask to know that my greatest work would live on in her voice.

129

This room that we rehearsed in had once been a part of a cave system; the limestone walls were rough – I had left them unfinished, as they naturally formed, in order to pre-serve the rich acoustics. The cavern was situated a few yards from my quarters, a location that approximated to the orchestra pit in the theatre ten metres above our heads. As I said, the sound in this chamber was astonishingly good, the dry air reverberated with song; the sand-textured walls were golden in the light from our torches. We were far enough beneath the surface for the sound to be muffled. I could commit a murder here, something long and drawn out, involving much screaming, and no one would be any wiser.

I ran my hands across the yellowish ivory keyboard, curs-ing my gloves for the difficulty they gave me, but I was unwilling to play bare-handed, exposing my mottled flesh to her sight. I struck a foul chord and the girl stopped short, halting mid-phrase. I turned to her and asked, 'Christine, could you start again at bar fifteen? I am uncertain of the phrasing. My gifts are as composer, not librettist.'

She laughed, tossing her dark hair, 'Of course, Erik. But I was wondering, if the emotion you're trying to convey is a sort of ominous fear, mingled with hope, shouldn't you change that note,' she pointed, to my copy of the manu-script, 'to A flat so that the strings will really leap when I sing, "Why have you brought me here, to the edge of the earth, where devils dance and angels tremble?"'

I stared at the text, considering. It just might work. I made the change, blotted the paper, then closed it back inside its book. We had been hard at work for five hours. Christine was ready for a rest, though she would never say so. Her sweat had soaked through the fibres of her rose-silk shirtwaist, her curls were damp against her forehead.

She had been with me nine days and it was remarkable to me how profoundly our relationship had changed.

She used my name so frequently, always with a slight smile on her lips, as though the sound of it filled her with some secret pleasure. For my part, I found myself confiding in her more than I ever thought possible. We talked together while she ate, lingering over her meals to draw the conversation out.

I found myself revealing things to her that I had planned to take to my grave.

That very morning we sat together over her breakfast, Christine had two slices of toast coated with honey and a carnelian apple that I cut for her, arranging the slices on a plate in a pattern that alternated deep red and stark white.

I have hated the smell of apples since my days in the carnival, but she asked for the fruit and so of course I provided it. I watched as she lifted the wedge to her mouth, watched her lips close around the bite, and I nearly shuddered. I would have thought that the mask I wore, the careful way I held my body, would have blocked her from perceiving my disgust.

Instead, she gave me a look so blatant in its perplexity that her face might as well have been a question mark. 'Erik, what is it? Is something wrong?' She looked at her plate, 'Is it the fruit?'

I held my hands in my lap, 'It is true, they are offensive. I despise them.'

Her head tilted to the side, as though she could see more of me by shifting her angle, 'Then why did you bring them?'

'Because you asked, and I would deny you nothing.'

'And so you cut them up for me, doing something that I could easily have done for myself, and then resented me for causing you to do it.' She suddenly seemed to find something interesting in the shining convex surface of her spoon.

I looked down at my hands, as though I could see the flesh, the blood beneath the kid-skin gloves. 'I do not resent you, Christine. The stench of the fruit seems to pull me backwards through time, to a place that I do not wish to revisit.'

'How could something so sweet, so natural, hurt you so?' She shook her head, then looked up and said, 'But then, the smell of the sea is like that for me, now. I used to smell it and think of the holidays that I spent with my father. Now I smell it and the memories are the same, but the context has changed. There is no sense of anticipation, only the ache of permanent loss.'

She reached across the table and laid her hand on the cloth so that her curled palm faced upward. I hesitated a moment, then placed my hand in hers. It took all of my courage not to withdraw when she squeezed it. This was the second time that we had done this. I must grow used to being touched.

She said, 'Tell me what happened.'

And so I did. God help me, I never expected to. I never wanted to burden her with it. The shame, the nakedness, the taunts. I told her what it was like to be on display, raw and filthy, to eat only what puerile people chose to pelt me with so that every meal came from, was formed from, my own humiliation. I told her what it was like to have my body splattered with the cores of apples that bounced from my skin and landed in a floor strewn with my own leavings which I could never clean because I was given enough water to wash myself or drink but never both. I told her about how I had to survive eating that fruit, filthy, crusted with bitterness.

I said, 'And all of this came about in payment for the crime of being born deformed.'

'You are deformed. That is no crime. You know that I will never run from you.' Her thumb tightened against the back of my hand, 'Let me ask you once more. Can you trust me enough to take off your mask?'

I tried to draw away from her, but could not. She refused to let go. Instead, she leaned across the table, looking through my eyeholes, trying hard to see behind them. I felt terror twining in my guts and my skin was suddenly drenched in foul-smelling sweat.

'Let me know what you are, Erik, let me see you. I love you, my teacher. Do not be afraid. I will not be frightened.'

I ran from her then, tearing my hand from hers and thrusting back against the hotel trolley so that it rolled into the wall, just missing her hip. She kept hold of the glove, peeled it from my hand so that my scarred white claw was exposed. Her face blanched when she saw it, that dead white thing, all the colour drained out of her soft cheeks. The expression on her face hit me like a blow to the chest; I had to get away from her. I had to make myself secure, get back to my rooms where I could breathe properly, and wait for the black edges of the world to regain their light.

I cannot forget the stricken look on her face as I left her, standing there in the middle of her bright room, holding my empty glove.

By the time that I returned that afternoon she had cleaned up the mess I'd made of her breakfast, washed the plates in her small sink and reordered the chairs around the trolley. My glove was lying on my seat, as though it were waiting for me. And as for Christine, she was waiting for me. She had changed into the shirtwaist that I had expressed a preference for and when I entered, bearing her lunch tray, she rose and apologised, 'for being so forward'.

I forgave her, of course. She could not help her reaction. After a few moments of awkwardness she ate the meal I served her, helped me clear away the dishes, then we both resumed our work.

12.

I have never been so close to happiness as I was then, that brief time twenty years ago when I lived with a woman who loved me and who shared in both my genius and the adoration of our work. We had three weeks together; a far cry from the six months that I had originally intended. Luckily the work moved very quickly – *Don Juan* was written by the time that we ended. She made her ascension after all, her glorious resurrection from the pit of the damned. It is not her fault if it did not go exactly as we planned.

Sitting here now, in the rooms that I have inhabited for nearly a third of a century, a chamber that might be a macrocosm of myself, among my papers, my books, and my new imported gramophone (I can listen to her voice whenever I wish, singing my songs. It's like having a captive ghost) it's almost possible to pretend that the past is really over, and that I have survived it.

As I get older I find myself turning for comfort to the stories of my childhood. Fairy tales that my mother never read to me, but which I consoled myself with over the long cold evenings in the cellar of the granite house my father built. I had a tattered copy of *La Belle et la Bête* my mother found in one of the rooms, left behind by a tenant. She had considered selling it, but in the end gave it to me in a gesture of strained love, or guilt. It was, for a time, my greatest treasure. I found hope inside its pages.

Reading it again now, a newer edition in buttery green-leather binding, I am struck by the way the myth reflects my story. All those nights that the Beast spent sitting across from the maiden, asking his questions and being rebuffed, only to win through in the end. I chose the word reflection carefully. Mirrors invert. His story is my story, subtly reversed.

We had our table with one place setting. The monster was there, and so was the maiden: the single red rose. But it was the maiden who asked for intimacy, over and over again, even when I begged her to cease. It was the Beast who refused transformation. It was the monster who, though strong enough to murder, turned and ran as fast as he could from the possibility of romance.

And so here I am, settled in the same leather armchair, growing older while my organ stands with the cover closed, the keys slowly shifting out of true as the wood decomposes, shrouded in a muslin tarpaulin. I rise, as thin as ever, maskless (I never bother with wearing it now) and set my recording of *Don Juan Triumphant* on the turntable.

Christine's voice rises up from the black wax grooves, her miraculous voice singing, 'Love is vanity, selfish in its beginning as its end, except where 'tis a mere insanity.' And I see her again, as fresh as the summer, a beautiful girl who sat by my side in her white dress, helping me to fit the music to the form.

We had been working in my rooms all morning; I had

brought a second chair to place beside my desk. Christine was wearing Marguerite's white dress; the costume had become a part of her wardrobe, and in truth it was exceptionally fetching, revealing the soft tops of her breasts and pale, gently muscled lengths of forearm. Books of poetry were open all around us. We were finishing the libretto for the final scene – the libertine who seduced Doña Ana was about to be dragged into Hell by the vengeful ghost of the poor maid's father.

Christine had developed a taste for the English poet Byron and she wanted to invert lines from the satire to serve our more serious purposes.

'What do you think of this?' she asked, tilting her head so that her curls spilled from her shoulders into her soft cleavage, '"The sun set, and up rose the yellow moon: The devil's in the moon for mischief", I was thinking that the servant Gato could sing that to the maid before the meal begins. It fits in well with the rhythm of the piece, and the image is certainly ominous enough.'

I nodded, 'Yes. And it foreshadows the ending of the story.' I sang the line, adopting a baritone based on the voice of the actor I hanged on her last night on the surface. Monsieur Jordan.

She laughed, clapping her hands like a child, and copied the words on to the composition paper. If you ever get a chance to examine the original score, I believe that it is currently housed in the Musée de la Musique, you will see a strange thing. The score seems to have been written in two different hands. One elegantly sets down the actual musical notation (the orders for *Timpani*, or *Allegretto* are rather spidery) the other, a strong, almost masculine calligraphy, transcribed the words. The styles are very different, and yet they exist in a state of absolute sympathy. To read the score for this *Don Juan* is to observe the perfect mingling of twinned spirits. It is beautiful to see.

Unfortunately the bound reproduction I have displays none of that. Printed, the genius of the piece, its passion, its experimental nature, shines through clearly, but it reads as though it were the product of one mind only; the twinned parts merge. Our wonderful unity is utterly masked.

We had only one full scene left to write; the aria that Doña Ana sings professing her love to the Don before he murders her father in the final act. We were having some difficulty capturing the spirit of the piece, transcribing the sense of what she felt, hopelessly waiting for the libertine to return her love. We read for a while, paging through my books in silence, when suddenly Christine's eyes lit up as though her spirit and her brain were blazing.

She stood before my chair, her hands clasped before her, and opened her mouth, singing, 'Give me the waters of Lethe that numb the heart, if they exist, I will still not have the power to forget you.'

For a moment I could not speak. It was so right for the scene. 'What was that?'

She looked at me, triumphant, her cheeks flushed, 'I found it in Ovid. *The Metamorphosis.*'

I stood on my uncertain feet, quite badly shaken. I took her hand. 'Close your eyes, Christine.'

Her body stiffened when I took hold of her arm, her fine face paled, but she did what I asked. 'Didn't you like it?'

I lifted my mask and kissed her, once, on her downy cheek. The pale flesh flared crimson where I had touched her, her full lips smiled. That is a sight that I will treasure for the rest of my life. Against every desire of my body, I drew back from her, once more lowering my false waxen face over the true. 'It was absolutely perfect.'

She opened her eyes; her look was languid, the pupils dilated, so that she seemed like a woman waking from a deep, sweet slumber. She stepped close to me and took both of my hands. Her voice had found a lower register, 'Erik…

And that was when we heard the crashing, the brittle crack of splintered wood and powdered plaster, the shouting of ten men battering through my false wall and clamouring down the narrow corridor towards the traps I'd set up between there and here. In that moment any possibility of our future happiness was shattered.

RAOUL

10.

I arrived at the Giry house at a little after midnight. My brother did not try to hinder me from pursuing my suspicions. He was too broken by his own loss. When the managers made their misguided attempt to bring me to reason, offering a dose of laudanum and a carriage ride to my own bed, my brother poured himself another brandy, leaned across the bar and said, 'I hope that you never have cause to test this, gentlemen, but believe me when I say that sometimes tilting at windmills can be the best balm for grief.'

His face was pouched beneath the eyes, his large nose red and clogged with tears; he looked so much older that I was suddenly struck by the resemblance he bore to our ancient father. He said, 'Give him the address; let him speak to the women. At worst, he will question them and learn nothing. At best he will thrash them with his words when what they tell him brings the sad truth home. Either way, he will heal all the faster.' Philippe shot the whole contents of the glass down his throat, sank into his chair and said in a quiet voice, 'God knows that I wish I had someone to scream at right now, someone to blame. As it stands, I cannot even truthfully slander myself.'

He buried his face in his hands.

Monsieur Andre opened a drawer in his desk, rifled through file cards. He copied down the address he found in a hand that shook and spattered the scrap he wrote upon with black drops of ink that resembled burnt gunpowder.

Few carriages remained outside the theatre. This was unsurprising considering the wreckage of the night. I passed the slow moving, exhausted groups of hospital wagons that, at this late hour, carried only the dead. A few firemen sat on the steps of the entrance sipping from a shared brown bottle, one child, splendidly dressed and as yet unclaimed by his surviving relatives, wept into his hands beneath the cart which bore the tank of water which finally extinguished the flames.

I clenched my jaws and walked even faster, considering the mind that could justify such waste. He did it all for the sake of pillage and capture. My will resolved itself. I owed a service to the world; I would track and slay the man who did this, even if I found that I had been mistaken about the identity of the headless corpse, even if Christine had died beneath the rubble. Someone, after all, had planted the bombs and planned the detonations. Someone had hanged the heavy baritone and taken the head off of an innocent girl, leaving her nameless.

And if, in the end, I found my love alive but ruined I resolved to swallow my disgust without ever showing her that I resented her for being spoiled. I would marry her in spite of it, if she still breathed, no matter what followed I would bring her home.

This was one promise I kept. I never knew that foulness could come wearing more than one form. I did not know that promises could be kept and broken all at once.

The neighbourhood that the Girys haunted was rough,

there were prostitutes about, beer halls, and no cabbies, but it was not nearly as decrepit as I'd expected. The shops were all filled with merchandise; no windows were broken. The houses were small, but most had been recently painted. Rubbish was in barrels, not scattered on the streets, and not even the few urchins I saw were picking through the bins for meals.

The slate steps for number 227 had been recently swept, the pot planted with daisies was watered, well-tended. Even in my rage, this residence was nothing like the one I would have imagined for the dwelling of a former convict.

I knew that, if my plan were to go forward, I could not reveal my conjectures to the women. I must approach this conversation as though I were honestly appealing to them for information, not accusing them of participating in the plot.

I found myself staring into the open face of a flower, suddenly supremely exhausted, focusing my energy on that golden glow as though I could fortify my soul with a fragment of beauty. I knocked on the door. Waited a moment hearing nothing but silence. I knocked again, harder.

After a few seconds I heard the clatter of feet rushing to the door.

'Who is it?' A rough girl's voice, a slight lisp, 'Don't you know it's after midnight?'

Little Meg. It had to be. So much for her supposed twisted ankle.

I answered in my most commanding tone, 'Madame, it is the Vis Comte de Changy. Open the door. I will speak to your mother.'

I heard the metallic clank of a drawn lock, the door drew open a few inches and the girl's dark, puckered face peered out. She examined me a moment, observed the street behind me, and drew the door closed long enough to unfasten the security chain. It must have been mounted fairly high on the beam, because the motion was accompanied with a series of acrobatic grunts and the sound of long-nailed fingers scrabbling on wood.

When she opened it again her face was flushed, she smiled at me through closed lips and stood aside for me to pass her, entering the hallway.

'It is a little late for visitors,' she said, leading me to the parlour to wait for her mother to make herself presentable. The girl was wearing a loose, flowered dress that flowed down to her ankles, her hands held tight together inside the deep pockets that pouched out the front of her pinafore. It was strange to see this tiny dancer dressed for sleep and not the stage. She looked so reduced, seen outside of her context.

'We can wait for her in here.' Keeping her hands where they were, she backed into the lip of the scrappy yellow sofa and hopped on to it, sliding her small bottom back onto the cushions in a motion that was obscene because it was so childish. 'Is this about the fire, then?'

I took the seat she offered, a rickety armchair that had obviously been rather a fine one, not so very long ago. 'You've heard about the fire then? You were very lucky to miss it.'

Her face snapped closed like a purse. 'I was unwell.'

I leaned forward into the stink of her breath. 'Then how did you come to hear of it?'

The girl was opening her ungodly mouth, ready to reply, when her mother answered for her. I had not heard her approach.

'La Carlotta was sitting in the audience when it

happened.' The older woman was standing in the doorway, fully dressed in her usual shabby black. 'She had not yet recovered her voice, but wished to see the show. About an hour ago she sent a boy with a note. Didn't you wonder why we answered the door at this late hour? We were upstairs, in great turmoil, only just beginning to undress again for sleep.'

The woman was tough; her hard face never flickered into smile or gained a softer expression. She sat on the couch besides her small daughter.

'Forgive me, Madame, if I say that seems uncommonly kind of her. I have never known a Diva to show such consideration for a box manager.'

The woman laid a gnarled hand on Little Meg's wildflower patterned knee. 'You have not yet offered tea to our visitor.'

The girl looked up at her, her expression blank. 'It is very late, Mother.'

I interjected, glad for a chance to get rid of the girl. She was very like a terrier. I addressed the mother. 'Tea would be lovely.'

She flicked her ringless finger towards the door. 'Go.'

The girl slid forward off of the sofa, her hands still hidden I wondered how she was planning to bear out the tray with her fingers shoved into her pockets.

The old woman sat silently for a few seconds, examining me. Finally she came to her decision and signalled with a smile that she was ready to talk.

'I am certain you know by now that I was a prostitute. Do not look so shocked, I hear all of the gossip.'

I closed my mouth.

She continued, 'You also know that I was jailed for the

offence, sentenced to a year or the payment of a large fine. I served three months before my darling daughter bought me out by selling her hair and teeth, her only physical beauties.' She sighed, 'Such a pity that only one of those gifts could ever come back to her.'

She smiled sadly at the sour memory of love, 'Have you never wondered, monsieur, how a woman like me could be trusted to gain a respectable position?'

In truth I had, and this was all very interesting, but I could not, for the life of me, see how it was connected to the matter at hand. When I told her so, she laughed, saying that I needed to learn how to listen.

She continued, 'After my release I went back to work – this was, you recall, five years ago, near the end of the siege, but the war was still raging.

'I was destitute. My daughter had begun ratting for the city ballet but there was little money in it. She earned a roof with her dancing, and when she was still a child, still growing, she learned to supplement her income by taking men into her bed.' Her face clouded then. 'It was very hard to watch. Thankfully, my luck changed soon. One of my regulars was the head architect of the Opera House, Monsieur Garnier, a brilliant gentleman who, though living in severely reduced circumstances and grieving himself over the abandonment of his building and the sudden death of his son, nevertheless found room for me in his heart. I became his mistress.'

She smiled at the recollection, a lip twitch in memory of happiness long spent, 'He would have married me, I am sure, but for my history and the fact that my first husband, Monsieur Giry, probably remains alive somewhere, though I have not heard from him since my Little Meg was an infant at the breast.

'As for my dear Charles, he died of consumption shortly after construction began again. It was lucky for me that he had many friends who respected him enough to leave aside their disgust at my past and offer me a job which paid enough in tips to allow my daughter and I to maintain our hold on the architect's house.'

She stood, ready to show me to the door. 'I trust that you are satisfied that neither my daughter nor myself would wreck the last visible structure that our saviour left upon the earth?'

I remained where I sat, unwilling to be ushered from her house. 'Madame, I never suspected that your fingers set those bombs beneath the stage, but...'

'Bombs?' She darted forward like a serpent, taking hold of my arm. 'There were bombs? My friend said fires only.'

I disengaged her fingers, 'Yes, Madame. Bombs. Dynamite. There was a tremendous explosion. Many were killed.' I rose now, sensing that it would be wise to intimidate her with a display of my masculine advantages of strength and height, 'There was also an abduction. My fiancée, Miss Daaé, was taken by the man who set this destruction in motion. He planned it all, as a means of capturing her.'

Her eyes grew wide, terribly frightened. She spoke one word, 'Erik?' Then fell silent.

Now I took hold of her, my hands on her shoulders. 'Erik? Is that the name of the fiend?' I was shaking her, without intending to. Her head lolled loosely on the stem of her throat. 'Her life, her innocent life is at stake, woman! You must tell me what you know.'

And that was when the girl, the loyal daughter, appeared in the doorway. She dropped the tray she was carrying and

I turned to look at her, shocked at the sound of fracturing crockery.

'Let go of my mother!' She shrieked at me, plunging her hands into her pockets.

I found that I could not loosen my grip on the old woman's throat. I watched the tea mingle with the teapot shards and seeped into the floorboards, spreading like dark urine across the floor.

Madame Giry gasped in my hands, 'Please!'

I ignored her, of course, much to my sorrow. The woman was obviously in deep shock and yet I shook her, striking her once or twice across the cheekbones, shouting, 'You must tell me who did this! I know that you know!'

Little Meg shouted at me once more, 'Stop! You are killing her!' and then she shot me through my centre. I heard the bullet enter before I felt any of the pain from it. I dropped the old woman and, I remember, she fell to a faint on the floor. I turned to Little Meg as I collapsed, the edges of the room darkening around me. I think that I was going to ask her a question. I noticed that she had torn the pocket of her dress when she pulled out the gun.

I woke up several days later, in the hospital. I had been found bleeding in the gutter, robbed of my money and my watch, a few short blocks from my house. The nursing nuns told me that it was very lucky that whoever had shot me had used faulty bullets. The shells had fractured as the gun fired. I was filled with shrapnel that I would carry for the rest of my life, but none of my organs had been punctured.

It took me nearly three weeks to recover. My brother visited often, but told me nothing about either the Girys or Christine, other than to let me know that the body that they took for hers, the headless mystery, had been given to the Countess who buried it next to the grave of the girl's violinist father in Brittany.

As for myself, I had almost accepted the loss of her, I had wept out my grief in an ocean of bandages brought by the nuns. It was not until I returned to the house of my brother that anyone thought to give me the letter that would change my life.

11.

I was unpacking the bags that Philippe had brought to comfort me in the hospital, shelving my favourite volumes of art reproductions and hanging my morning jacket on the handle of the wardrobe to be taken away and washed.

I had to stop and massage the sealed scar besides my navel, the site where most of the lead shards sliced their way into my belly. That damned girl. I do not know what held me from reporting her to the police to be properly tried.

No that is a lie. I knew, I know. It was pity for the mother.

When I first woke from the surgery I felt such a surge of wrath at her, the likes of which I had never experienced before. The nursing nuns were very frightened at the violence of my incoherent shouting. Thinking that I was experiencing heart failure or succumbing to stress-induced brain fever they fetched the surgeon who spoon-fed me morphine until I slept beyond the boundaries of rage, grief, or physical agony.

When I woke I was considerably calmer. I had dreamed about her, you see. Madame Giry. I saw her sitting in that filthy cell, trapped and weeping, while the only person left in the world who loved her mutilated herself to effect a rescue.

I knew that I had succumbed to violence against the dancer's mother, and that my actions were inexcusable. It must have been very frightening for Little Meg when she found us. The girl, it seemed, was protecting her still. It was almost as though their roles had been reversed; the mother was in the keeping of the daughter.

So I let them go. I told the police that I remembered nothing of the night of the fire, and bent my will to my recovery.

This was the first time that I had ever thought about a whore, about the misfortunes that could drag a woman to such sin. I have never forgotten it, and to this day I do not regret protecting them.

I sat down on my bed, thrusting the thick curtains aside and fingering my belly. I had just resolved to take another swallow of laudanum and fall into a grief-dissolving dream, (a habit that I have lately resumed) when there was a knock on my door.

'Come!' I ordered.

A servant entered, a new girl that I had never seen before. Apparently the woman she replaced had been there that night, in the pit-audience. She never emerged.

This girl, a thin twelve-year-old in a too-large dress and a cap that slid over her eyes, curtsied once and handed me a thick letter. 'This came for you, sir. While you were in hospital.'

I had nothing to tip her, so I thanked her with a smile and she fled, disappointed, flouncing her skirts. I could hear her muttering against me in the hallway.

I examined the envelope. It was made from a single sheet of paper that had been folded and glued. It was cheap foolscap made from badly processed pulp, flecks of wood were visible in the grain. There was no postal mark, it must have been delivered in person. My name, scrawled across the front in an uncertain hand, was the only identifying feature.

I sliced it open with my fingernail, unwilling to wait long enough to search my desk for my penknife or a letter-opener.

I found two folded sheets of that same cheap paper. They were scrawled all over, front and back, with words that were so tightly packed that they were just barely legible.

Dear Monsieur Changy,

I would like to apologise for the actions of my daughter, and for our treatment of you after your unfortunate accident. When Meg saw the way you handled me she was severely disturbed. You see, she has no malice in her, but rather she acted out of pure love for her mother.

I thank you, also, for not reporting us. I know that you refrained because if you had not the police would have been here already and they have not come. You see, I have been to jail, and I know that they treat the women that land there much worse than they do the men. The police seem to see violence in men as a natural part of all their natures, an understandable lapse. They see women as something other than themselves, something delicate and pure, incapable of anger. When women act in the same way as men they must be monsters, abominations. Not at all like their wives who never even dare to speak back to them. And so we are more harshly punished.

I was, anyway. You would not believe the beatings that I have taken.

But enough of that. I wrote to thank you, not blather, and I wish to repay your kindness in whatever way that I can.

When you told me that the fire was not caused by arson,

but rather had been set by a series of explosions your words stirred up memories that I believed I had forgotten. I do not know if I would have told you this before, had things ended more amicably between us, but now I find myself in your debt. Luckily I can pay you with words that my darling daughter would see as a betrayal of the only father that she ever knew. But my darling Charles is dead and long-since in heaven where he can feel no woe and there can be no betrayal, for in death there are no secrets anymore.

Do you remember what I told you that night? How, when we came together, he was grieving for two losses; his son and the Opera House? Well, as the years passed and we grew closer he told me a little more.

The man who died was no more his natural son than Meg was his daughter, but Charles had raised him from boyhood and taught him his art. I have seen similar bonds form among dancers. The truest parent of an artist is often the one who discloses to them the secrets of creation. He had, it seems, lost the boy once before. Charles told me that the lad had been stolen from him and sold to a carnival or travelling circus. He was, apparently, quite deformed ... though Charles never spoke of that. He had no images of Erik. I cannot tell you what he looks like.

In any case, my lover said that the boy never fully recovered from the years he spent as a captive before his father found and rescued him. He had become quite violent – apparently he would strike a mason across the face for marring a brick. When he disappeared, along with the other architects who worked under him, Charles at first suspected the soldiers who at that time flooded the streets with their mischief.

That was all I knew for many years. My Charles died, as I told you, and in pity I was given the job which now supports us.

Almost as soon as the theatre opened there were rumours

of a ghost. Letters appeared, addressed to the managers in a frightening hand like that of a demented child who learned to write with ash and splinters...

My mind flashed back to the note I found in Christine's chambers. The love letter sealed with the lyre of Orpheus.

...demanding extortionate payment in return for protection against misfortune against the scenery and cast.

The managers refused, of course. Those men like to think of themselves as reasonable men. But when the Opera House opened and entire acts were marred by tripping dancers, falling scenery, and in one instance all of the boxes had to be closed because something that looked like blood came pouring out of the walls, Firmin and Andre rethought their position.

I am telling you all of this because I suspect that the missing son, that Erik, remains at the bottom of this. He was an architect; he had supervised the construction of buildings. He would know how to use dynamite to level foundations. I also remember something strange that happened once, when Charles was still living.

He was taking me round the unfinished theatre – it felt like a ruin, so dusty, already haunted – we had already seen the stage, those wonderful frescoes, I saw the seats lined up against the wall, still sealed in their boxes. We were leaving through the back door, passing the rehearsal rooms, the dressing chambers that no star had ever sung in, on our way to the manager's office when suddenly he stopped and wheeled to what appeared to be an unbroken marble panel of wall.

He ran his hands over it, as though seeking something. Then he turned to me and said, 'My dear, this is very perplexing. In the plans we made I remember that Erik included a doorway here, with stairs leading down to the basement. We had meant to include some more rehearsal and storage rooms, as well as a sauna and bath house for the richer clientele.'

I was growing bored by then I said, 'Maybe they changed it.'

He said, 'No, no. Erik insisted that it be included.' He smiled at me, 'That boy always insisted that every building have a basement as complex as the room visible on top. It was a quirk of his.'

And with that, our tour concluded. I took him home. That same week the first spots of blood showed up on his handkerchief and I forgot all about our tour. That is, until the strange haunting began and I discovered that no one had ever seen the rooms he mentioned. In fact, hardly anyone has ever been into the basement.

And so, Monsieur, my advice to you is to begin there. Seek out the panel he mentioned. Go down, carefully. If Erik did take your girl, that is where he fled with her. Remember that he is dangerous. Go armed, and not alone.

There. I had a debt to you, once. I have paid it.

My daughter and I wish nothing but the best to you, we wish you luck. Please leave us alone.

Sincerely,
Anne Giry

I finished the letter, thought a moment, adjusting the pillows behind my head. I sent the servant for my brother.

After he had finished reading, the disbelief draining from his face along with his blood, he was white with rage and as angry as I was. He agreed to my plan almost immediately. It took the rest of the evening to seek and hire enough armed men to go after the monster. We did not wish to involve the police in order that we might spare Christine the scandal and Madame Giry another cycle of the year in jail. In the end we managed it. It was fortunate that the city was filled with unemployed soldiers itching for work. We set the time of our attack for early the next evening, after the repair work had concluded for the day and the workers had departed.

My brother contacted the managers as a courtesy. They gave their blessing, free reign of the theatre and access to tools, but they did not wish participate in the actual rescue, though they hoped that I would find my fiancée alive, well, and still fit for marriage.

Philippe at first tried to dissuade me from joining the raid, citing my injury, but he recognised that, like him, I was burning with vengeance.

'I must be the one to rescue Christine.' I told him, raising my body from my bed. 'She will be my bride yet!'

He nodded once, bitterly smiling, and left me to rest.

It took me longer than usual to fall asleep. In the end I resorted again to the laudanum. I slept well, and woke late. By mid-afternoon I was more than ready to begin.

12.

We had some difficulty, at first, locating the entrance to the monster's lair. The wall seemed to be constructed from a solid sheet of marble, impeccably smooth to the touch. We had only Madame Giry's vague instructions to begin our search and I admit that (being young) I was easily frustrated. I paced the corridor, stalking back and forth across the tiles, while the former soldiers slumped against the walls gossiping and shooting dice.

It was Philippe's idea to apply method to the search. Beginning directly outside of the door marked 'Managers:

Firmin & Andre' my brother laid his ear to the wall and knocked, listening for the echo of reverberation. He repeated this every few feet until he stopped short, halfway down the corridor. He looked up, excitedly whistled; a shrill, high pitch that drew me to his side in a flurry. 'Raoul, lay your head here.'

I did as he said and I heard the echo of his knocks for myself. Straightening again, my hand on the handle of my revolver, I said, 'To be sure, it is hollow, but it looks exactly like the rest of the wall. How can we be certain that there is a passage?'

My brother smiled and guided my hand to a nearly imperceptible crack, straight as a knife-edge, that ran vertically from floor to ceiling. It was invisible to the eye, or nearly, but my touch recorded it. He said, 'There is another exactly like it two and a half feet over. Doesn't that sound right for a doorway?'

I returned his grin and together we began pressing and prying at the doorway until my fingers caught on a catch, a secret lever, made to look like a flaw in the marble. When I pressed this irregular protrusion the wall slid outward an inch and a half, revealing the doorway. I hooked my hands inside the blackness and pulled.

There was no stairway. There was no corridor.

All I saw was lathe and plaster, a dead-end!

I cried out in frustration, a sound which drew the soldiers from their game and caused my brother to place his restraining arm around my shoulders. I shook him off and struck the wall, belting out my rage at it until the dust flew and my sweat and saliva flowed. I was weeping without realising it, unconsciously pawing the tears from my eyes with the backs of my fists until I sank to the floor, exhausted.

The soldiers were staring at me; eight pairs of eyes convinced that I was mad. Only my brother failed to look at me. He was examining the wall that I had attacked, wiping away flecks of blood and shattered splinters to reveal a hole that opened like an eye into the kingdom of death.

'Ah, my clever friend, now we have you!' He picked up one of the axes we had brought and struck at the lathes. Instead of the struggle we expected, the whole wall fell forward, a door-sized plug that shattered to splinters on the stairs. The soldiers raised their voices, cheering, shouldering their guns and adjusting their knives in their belts. My brother came to me where I was sitting and offered me his hand, 'Come on, Raoul. Let's go and rescue your bride.'

With lit torches in hand, we plunged into the dark. It did not escape my notice that the stairs were nearly exactly the same, in materials and composition, as the grand entrance of the Opera House; albeit on a smaller scale. They were like fingers on the same hand, all of a piece. This building really was the product of a single mind – and it did not belong to Charles Garnier.

Our torchlight danced on the walls. As we descended past the typical basement brick, sinking into the bedrock, the corridor opened out until by the time the staircase ended we found ourselves inside a vast, black cavern. It was very like a cave, a natural formation. Our torches were not bright enough to light the walls, so we walked amidst a wealth of shadow. Somewhere out of sight we heard the sound of water dripping. After what felt like an hour, but must have really been only a few minutes, we came to a wall that opened up into three doors that hung with an inch or so of open space above the earth-strewn floor.

I paused for a moment, holding up my hand. 'We need to make a decision. A monster is in here, somewhere. We need to know which way to go.' This was like one of the fairy tales Christine's father told us when we were still children. A monster, a princess, a castle underground. I knew that I was being tested. I hoped so much to pass.

One of our men, a rough-looking fellow with an eye-patch and a ragged vest, said, 'The floor is pretty muddy. We had better look for tracks.'

After a few minutes he found some, a single set of man-sized prints leading into the centre doorway. I moved to open it, but he hesitated, holding on to my arm. He scratched his stubbled chin and said, 'Now wait a minute, sonny.' He flinched, 'I mean "Sir". You say this fella's pretty smart?'

I nodded.

He continued, 'Well, this patch of earth has tracks in it, sure enough, nice clear ones leading you on, almost like an invitation.'

My brother came and faced him, 'What are you saying, Jacques?'

He smiled, revealing two chipped front teeth stained brown by tobacco, 'Well, you said he brought a lady with him, right? Well it stands to reason that, unless he was carrying her (and the prints aren't sunk in deep enough for that) he must have led her by the hand. So we should be seeing two sets of prints. One walking, one set being dragged. And there aren't any here.'

I opened my mouth to speak my frustration. Before I could say anything another soldier, this one short, dark haired, and very broad, gave a whistle and called us over to the door on the left. When we got there he smiled and held his torch as close as he could to the earthen floor. It had been swept. The short man had a bass voice. He said, 'It looks like someone's been covering his tracks.'

However intelligent our quarry, he'd had little experience with hunters.

We opened the door.

It was only much later that I learned how lucky we were. Christine told me afterwards that the middle path was armed with buried explosives, so that an ill-placed foot would lead to an instant, or a very painful death.

This path was long, circuitous, rather like the circuit of a nautilus; we wound round the Opera House several times in our journey to the centre, but our work was made easier by the fact that fiend had only swept up to the door, beyond it the two pairs of tracks were bright in the torchlight; his long and firm, moving at a rapid pace, hers, small and fine, with the occasional scuff-mark where she had tripped or been dragged. There were many doors, many off-shooting hallways, but we took none of them, trusting that the path we pursued would lead us to her.

Most of the rooms we passed through were unfinished, composed of stone walls and floored with dirt, but the circular route we followed was leading us directly under the Opera House and the closer we came to the centre the more civilised the rooms. They sprouted plaster walls and floor tiles, scattered bits of furniture and other evidences of inhabitation so that, by the time we came to the room with the well, we had almost begin to relax.

This was a plunge back into darkness, a reversion to the stone and earth we encountered when we first left the staircase. The stench was abhorrent, fish left out too long in sunlight, rotten flesh. I gagged, choked back my vomit. The source of the odour was soon apparent. The floor was stacked with bodies, three skeletons that the water had rotted lay in a row along the floor. A fresher corpse was collapsed in the corner, his neck encircled by a rotting noose. Beside this was the much fresher head of a woman with long blonde hair, the eyes sunken in. The rest of her was buried in a bone yard in Brittany.

I nudged Philippe when I saw that. He nodded, held his hand up for silence, gesturing with the other one to a door across the room.

There was the faint sound of voices. I crept towards the entrance, the others trailing behind me. The portal was refined, polished mahogany, incongruous to the room. I lay my ear against it, listening. I heard her voice! She was alive!

I beckoned the others forward, listening as hard as I could. I was unable to make out exactly what she said, the wood was too thick and she was speaking too quietly. But I heard the fiend as clearly as though he were speaking by my shoulder.

'They will be here any minute.' I recognised the powerful voice of Christine's mysterious tutor! 'I must be ready for them.'

She said something then, softly, so softly. She must have been weak. The monster might have been starving her.

'No. We would have heard the explosions. They must have found the safe path. The very devil must be giving them luck! But the angels themselves are on our side, my dear, I have…'

I'd heard enough. I pulled back from the doorway, looked to my men. My brother smiled at me, clapped his hand on my back. I treasure that look. It was the last one we had.

We opened the door and walked into a room as bright as daylight. In the centre, beside an enormous, obscene bed, the monster stood with his hand on my lady.

CHRISTINE

13.

When he kissed me I knew that I was wrong. Not about everything, I still believe that I was right in trying to extricate myself from Raoul, and the time that I had spent underground perfecting my art and helping Erik to compose his masterpiece was the best and most fruitful period of my life. Then or since. No, I learned that I was wrong about what my master was to me.

He was not the ghost of my father. He loved me, as my father did, but his love was not pure in its source or filial in its expression. He did not love like an angel would, at a distance; he wanted my flesh as well as my spirit, no matter how hard he tried to deny it to himself. I decided then that I would help him to realise it.

Of course I was frightened of the things that he hid from me, beneath his mask, his gloves, his terrible history. He had killed before and showed no repentance for it. He would do so again. I was young enough, then, to believe that I could show him another way. And who knows? If events had played out just a little differently I might have had the chance.

I did not know it, but I had reached the high point of my life, standing there in that sweat-stained white costume

159

exhausted and exalted all at once while he ordered me to close my eyes and touched me with his naked lips. And that is so pathetic I could scream.

It only lasted a second, and when I opened my eyes he had lowered his mask and was standing a full foot away from me, as though he had appalled himself. I stepped toward him and spoke, 'Erik,' I have no idea what I would have followed, what I would have said given the chance. Whatever it was, I was interrupted by the sound of a crash as the barrier came down. It was the invasion of our world.

He stepped around me, moving as swiftly as the deadly butterfly knife that Little Meg carried in her cleavage, placing himself between my body and the door.

'Erik?' I touched his shoulder, felt his bones shift, his ropy muscles stiffening beneath the silk suit he wore. 'What is it?'

He turned to me. Behind his mask his flat yellow eyes seemed suddenly to glow. 'They are coming for you, Christine. Your would-be fiancée comes to your "rescue".' He took my hand. His own was trembling. 'They are not taking the route that I would have had them choose, we would have heard the explosions by now.'

He looked to the door, as though expecting them to defy physics as easily as they defied our plans and materialise immediately in the hallway. His voice sounded dead, defeated already. 'I could let you go, now. Feign a change of heart and give you to him. That would certainly be easier, and we would both be allowed to live.' He said these things, even as he squeezed my hand tighter, even as he shook with grief at the thought. 'Or we could fight. Head them off. I could kill them. Then we could remain together and continue our work, and you would be reborn to the world as a singer.'

I looked at him, raised my free hand to the side of his mask as though it were his real cheek that I were cupping and not a painted model made of wax. It was as warm as flesh. 'Fight. I have never known the easy path to be the best one.'

Erik hugged me, close enough to smell the foulness seeping through the seams of his clothes. I drew back, continuing, 'Fight, I say, but try not to kill them. There has been enough death.'

You see, I was already trying to change him.

He agreed to it, however, promised to avoid a slaughter if he could. And that is how I doomed us both.

'Come.' He pulled me to the closet at the other end of his chambers and motioned for me to sit on his bed. I was too surprised to be scandalised. I sank, a little, into the feather mattress. He opened the door, revealing a small room with (of all things) a long mirror at the end. There, among his clothing, his costumes, was a large trunk carved of rosewood. He flung open the lid, lifted out folded carpets, some curious porcelain oriental figures, and a small ebony box inlaid with fine shards of mother of pearl and ivory. Turning to me, he said, 'You have seen my store of explosives. Those are deadly. These begin from the same source but the effect is different. Those explosions cause a bloody death. The bombs in this box bring only sleep. It will not be the sweetest slumber of their lives, but it will have the properties of Lethe.'

He opened the lid, revealing balls the size of cherries wrapped in black paper, a wick protruding like a stem. I could smell them from here, a perfume like Attar of Roses, a bitter bite underneath. 'They will wake eighteen hours later, perhaps in the market near the Seine, and they will discover that the last week of their lives has become a blank.'

I smiled at him, 'That sounds perfect.'

He stood, 'Yes. I should have thought of it sooner.' Taking my hand, he helped me to stand.

'What will happen, after?'

'I have no idea, child.' He laughed a little, 'But we will have the better part of the day to work it out. If they are coming by the safe route then they will emerge in your room. The ventilation in there is good; I can use these little bombs without risk to ourselves. Still, just in case, you had better wet a handkerchief and tie it around your nose and mouth to serve as a filter to breathe through. Do it now, they might move faster than we think and if they do I will have to risk throwing it, no matter where we are.'

I took the scarf he offered, immaculately white, and did what he asked.

'But what about you, Erik?' When I spoke my voice was muffled, though understandable. I wondered how he managed to sound so clear even with a constantly covered mouth.

'My mask is lined with cloth, it will serve the same purpose.'

In less than a minute we were in my rooms, standing beside the beautiful bed that he made for me from marble and rugs.

I asked, 'How much time do we have?'

'They will be here any minute.' He walked to the door that they would enter through, counting his paces to calculate his throw. 'I must be ready for them.'

When he returned to me he held three of the small bombs in one hand, a Lucifer match in the other, ready to light the fuses.

Anxiety was gnawing at my stomach like a rat. I had to tell him, I couldn't tell him. 'Erik, I am afraid. What if they really did make it through one of the other doors?'

'No. We would have heard the explosions. They must have found the safe path.' He touched my shoulder with the hand that held the matches, brushing my hair from my neck, 'The very devil must be giving them luck! But the angels themselves are on our side, my dear, I have…'

And that was when the door opened. The first face I saw was Raoul, leading the others, his handsome young features looking older and drawn, whitely furious. Absurdly, I noticed that he'd shaved his moustache, that he was bleeding from the knuckles. It took me what felt like forever to notice that he was holding a gun.

His brother, Comte Philippe, had a revolver, too. The eight men they brought were armed with knives and firearms all their own.

They came to us armed, as though chasing an animal. And I had asked Erik to spare them.

My lover stepped in front of me, in one fluid motion pushing me slightly to the side so that I stood on the marble lip of the tub that I slept in. He struck a Lucifer on the side of his mask, lighting it and marring the finish, lighting the fuses of the three bombs he held as the invaders raised their guns to fire.

He threw them quickly, the bombs already smoking. Fear flooded my mouth like the taste of new coppers and I grew drunk on the stench of roses.

Guns went off as the bombs fell. I could not see who fired. Erik leapt backwards, aiming low, hooking his arms around my belly and diving with me into the bed where we landed. I was too shocked to struggle as he buried me in blankets, blinding me with velvet, shielding me from danger.

The room was full of shouting for a moment, and then drenched in stillness that hit us like a flood of water. I felt Erik's body pressing mine down, felt him moving, and then heard his voice speaking right next to my ear as his old ventriloquist tricks returned for the final act.

'Keep perfectly still, as though you were a corpse.'

And then he was gone. I heard him climbing up the side of the pool, heard the sound of his feet gaining traction on tile. I heard him as he muttered, a meaty thump that must have been the sound of him testing the awareness of our attackers with a well-placed kick.

'Christine!' His voice, so jubilant, 'All is well. You can come out now!'

I was doing just that, untangling myself from the blankets he had shielded me with, when I heard Raoul's voice shouting, 'Monster!'

I hurried to my feet, trying to stand, failing, frightened by the sound of struggle going on above me. I tried again and this time I rose, in time to hear the report of a gun, the crack of a bullet shattering tile, a loud clatter.

By the time I pulled my head above the rim the main part of the battle was over. The floor was littered with bodies. Most of the men had stopped in terror as their corner of the room filled with smoke, and that doomed them. They breathed in the smoke, and they fell. Raoul had been different. He told me, later, that the sight of 'the monster's' hand on my shoulder had filled him with an incredible rage. When the smoke flooded the room, he hadn't been breathing. He ran right through it, firing his gun.

When we plunged into the pool a wave of dizziness hit

him and he fell, for a moment, beside my wash-basin, well away from the lingering fumes. When Erik emerged, Raoul was just gaining consciousness. His memory was not impaired in any way, though he felt unbalanced and terribly ill. He bided his time until Erik kicked his brother in the side, testing the drug's effectiveness. The sight of that shining shoe connecting with Philippe's fat ribs reignited Raoul's rage and sent him leaping at my teacher, gun drawn, then blazing.

The first bullet missed, hitting the tile. Erik had inhaled none of his drug, he was clear headed and quick as ever. He struck the gun from Raoul's hand with a well-placed strike at the younger man's wrist, but that was not enough to incapacitate a boy just entering his prime, even if he was still recovering from an injury.

Raoul leapt at him, snarling, pinning him down on the tiles.

This is what I saw when I raised my head above the tiles.

Erik was lying face-down on the floor, panting loudly, his hands pinned behind him. Raoul was sitting on his spine, digging his knees into the thinner man's kidneys. Their heads were pointed in my direction; my master was looking at me, sorrowfully, silently. Raoul was cursing. The white scarf I'd been using as an air-filter had tightened in the struggle. It was wedged between my teeth so that I could not speak. Frantically, I moved to untie it so that I could shout to Raoul (he hadn't seen that I had risen yet), I would take this gag off, undo the knot. I would beg him to let Erik live.

But then I heard a voice, very soft, behind my left ear. 'No Christine, no. Remain perfectly still. Do nothing. I love you too well to see your life ruined.'

What could I have done, but obey him?

Besides, by then Raoul had seen me. His blue eyes blazed with the mixture of fury and possessive wrath at a theft that he called love. He tied Erik's hand with a rope he had carried, attached to his belt, dragged him from the ground so that he was standing and bound him to the nearest marble pillar, looping the rope around a mounted lamp so that his hands were held above his head.

When he had finished with that he returned to me, lifting me out of my bed and setting me gently down in a chair near the door. My body felt very cold, just then, and though I was sweating I was also shivering, so badly in fact that when Raoul untied the gag from my mouth my teeth began chattering so hard that they hurt.

Seeing this, Raoul went to the bed and returned with a blanket that he tucked around me. His touch was repugnant, my skin crawled receiving it, but I could not move, could not fight him in any way, not even when he used his bloody fingers to smooth back my hair.

I was so frozen with fear, with exhaustion, that I could not scream when he kissed me on the forehead.

I wish that I had fainted, then. I wish that I had lost myself to the world, that I had breathed in some of Erik's smoked Lethe or tasted another sip of his sleeping cordial, before I witnessed what followed. But I was awake, and aware, though unable to move. This is what I saw, then. I saw Raoul check his brother's pulse and, satisfied that he lived, I watched as he plucked the gun from his hand.

I watched him cock a bullet into the chamber.

I watched him walk to my master as he hung from the pole, his arms visibly straining, nearly screaming in their sockets.

I watched Raoul lift the barrel so that it was pointing

into the socket of the mask, the oiled metal nearly touching the flat eye of the man that I loved.

I saw Raoul's finger tighten on the trigger, then release the pressure before the shot was fired. He lowered the muzzle, looked back at me, and asked, 'Do you not wish to look upon the face of your abductor?'

With one fluid motion, hooking his fingers into the space where wax met the pale skin of Erik's chin, Raoul tore it away in one fluid motion.

The mask was off; Erik's terrible face was exposed. I felt my afternoon meal churning in my guts, and then I vomited the contents across the floor tiles.

14.

The mask was off. Raoul held it in his hand. The black wig that Erik wore over it had fallen to the floor. The face beneath seemed hardly human – much more resembling the desiccated face of a mummy than the flesh of a living man. He had barely enough skin to cover his skull. There were lips, of course, he could sing and speak without impediment, but they were shrunken, dry slits that could not totally cover his huge white teeth. Instead of a nose there was a gaping, moist-looking hole that provided the only colour on his face. It reminded me of a leaf-nosed bat that I'd seen a picture of in a book once, an image that frightened me so badly that I could never stand to look at it again. His cheeks and scabrous skull were covered with dried lesions and scars that had healed badly, long ago.

But worse than all of this, by far, were his eyes. They were sunken deep into the orbits of his skull, like those of a week-old corpse that had been left out in the sun. His lids were not sufficient to cover them totally so that when he closed his eyes now, to escape my horror-look, the effect was even worse than it had been before. The yellow gleamed through the gaping lids, seeming to invite the scavenger birds to come and peck.

And yet, they were sentient. I had to remind myself. Those eyes looked at me and knew me, loved me, and that knowledge struck me like a knife. I wiped my reeking mouth with the back of my hand, knowing that if I could only stand to love a mask it wasn't love at all but a delusion unworthy of enduring.

The strange spell that had held me to the chair, the shock of sudden cold and trembling, had passed. I found that I could move. I tried to speak, 'Erik.'

I had forgotten about Raoul.

The young man was still standing there, holding the mask in one hand and the revolver in the other, aiming the black muzzle into his captive's chest. When I spoke he wheeled round to face me, dropping the mask to the floor with a clatter. He said, 'Close your eyes, Christine.'

I saw him bring his foot down on to the face that I knew, deforming the wax with the weight of his body, destroying it irreparably. It flattened, then shattered. He said, 'Close your eyes. I'm going to get rid of the monster. You don't need to see this.'

How could I have stopped him? I was totally unarmed. True, the fallen men around me had hold of their guns, but when I tried to rise and reach them my legs gave way beneath me and I fell to the ground. The sound that I made, landing on tile, distracted Raoul. He turned to see what had happened to me, jerking as he squeezed the trigger so that the barrel pulled a little to the left as it fired. Not that it did any good for Erik.

I saw a gout of blood burst from the new hole beneath his ribs, I smelled the burnt stench of cordite and smelled something terrible, like a dead rat with a burst stomach split by the sun on the sidewalk. I tried to scramble to my feet again, my legs felt like blocks of wood beneath my white skirts.

Raoul looked at Erik, face flooded with disgust, about to fire at him again. I called out to stop him, 'Raoul, no! Help me!' I gave into my weakness.

The boy shoved the still-smoking gun into his belt and left the body where it hung. He came, running, to my aid, taking me in those well-formed arms of his and laying kiss after kiss on my cold, wet face. I had no idea that I was weeping until I saw the glimmer of my tears on his red lips. He stroked my hair, drew me up into the heat of his body, so that I leaned against him as we sprawled across the floor.

'Christine, Christine, you can stop shaking.' He rocked me in his arms like a colicky child, 'The monster is dead, and you are safe now. You are safe, and pure, and we shall be married. You'll leave here with me, I'll carry you, we'll go out and get help for my brother and the men.'

I could not take my eyes off the corpse.

Raoul struggled a little, lifting me back into the chair. He was winded and still aching from his wound. He would need assistance rescuing his men. I watched him thinking, pacing the floor between Erik and myself, coming to conclusions. Finally he stopped and turned to me, 'I'm going to need some help, my darling. You cannot walk yet, you cannot come with me. The monster is dead. You are safe now.' He looked to the lightly breathing bodies on the floor, 'My brother will need a doctor's care.'

He came to where I was sitting, lifted my hand to his lips, 'Christine, my darling, I must leave you here for a few minutes. One of the doors we passed opened out on to the street. I must go there and get help. Any help I can. I will have to leave you here for a few minutes.'

I shook my head, how could I remain in the same room as the body of the man that I had betrayed with my silence?

'Christine, you'll be safe, I swear it. You will be safe. I will not be more than a few minutes.' And with that, he left me, fleeing through the doorway he had entered through into the darkness, seeking out the light again.

I knew that I did not have more than a quarter of an hour. Raoul was moving quickly, spurred by grief and fear. Soon this cavern would be filled with people, prying eyes, policemen. They would take Erik's body, drag it into the daylight, naked. I could not allow that to happen. I had to make a decision.

I forced myself to stand, expecting to find myself sprawling again. My legs held. Somehow I made it over to the pillar he was pinned against. I hate to admit that I was fighting my own repugnance at the sight of him. Every step I took forward I had to force. And then, when I got there, I had to look. You see, I thought I owed him that much at least, an unflinching, unafraid look, into his eyes. It almost didn't matter that he couldn't see it.

And then I closed my eyes, strained my body up on tiptoes, and kissed him once upon the lips. Blind, they felt human. They tasted sweet, still warm.

I drew back, as though burnt. I thought I felt a breath between them.

I reached forward, touched his neck. There was a slow, strong pulse.

Examining the wound I saw that the bullet had passed through the flesh above his left hip and exited again, lodging in the tile behind him, sundering a painted Krishna from his woman. There was a chance, a small one, that it had not pierced any major organs, that the stench of death that emerged from the wound was just the odour of himself.

Moving in a panic now, I fetched the chair and stood upon it and undid the rope that bound him to the wall-sconce. I used a paring knife from the hotel trolley to split the strands and left it there, in a pile with the rope. Erik was very thin, I did manage to catch hold of him beneath the shoulders and lower him to the ground without either dropping him or getting much blood on to me. I could not lift him, I wasn't strong enough.

I laid him out flat onto the tiles, lifted his jacket and shirt up far enough to expose the wound. It was clean, like a cored apple. I fetched the scarf that I had used to bind my mouth and wet it again in the water from the basin. I used this to bind the wound, hoping that it would stop the bleeding, I pulled it as tight as I could. I watched the white scarf turn red. It would have to be enough.

There was no place I could drag him but my bed, so that was where I took him. I drew him the few feet across the floor, entering the depression and hauling him in after me. Once he was settled I checked his breathing – still strong – and before I covered him, while there was still time, I ran to my desk and wrote him a note. Ten words on a white slip of paper that I folded into his pocket before covering him up with layers of silk rugs.

I knew my time was very brief now. I had to hurry. I scrambled out of my bed to cover my tracks. Thank God, there weren't many. A few smears of blood on the floor, easily wiped up. I was disposing of the rag I'd used when I heard Raoul coming at the head of what sounded like a small army of men. Knowing that I would have to answer fewer questions if he seemed to find me unconscious, I sprawled out face down on the floor and began breathing shallowly. It was only half acting. I was beyond exhausted.

I heard the boy cry out when he saw me, felt him lifting me into my arms, checking my face, my throat, laying kisses on my eyelids. I opened my eyes to put a stop to it.

The fear fled his face, the ruddy colour coming back to it. He spoke to the people who had followed him into the room, 'She's alive! He did not kill her in his escape!'

A shadow fell over me, a middle-aged policeman hunkering down to speak, 'The fiend is not here! Are you certain that you shot him?'

Raoul looked angry for a moment, gestured over to the pillar. 'You'll see his blood there. The place where the bullet passed through his body. There is a hole in the wall.'

A deputy, I knew his rank by the small size of his hat, examined the wall and said, 'The lad's right, sir! This pillar is all bloody. And look,' he lifted up a piece of rope, the pearl-handled paring knife, 'this is how he done it! He must have had the knife up his sleeve the whole time. He must have been waiting for this opportunity.'

The Chief looked at me with new respect, laying his fat hand onto Raoul's shoulder, he said, 'Your fiancée is an incredibly lucky lady.'

Raoul hugged me close to his breast, rocking me gently. 'Yes, she is. We both are.'

The police searched the rooms, as far as they dared to, but of course no one thought to examine my bed. I asked the officer who searched Erik's room to fetch me the folder

he found there, a black bound thing, full of musical notations: the full score of Don Juan, nearly completed. I hid it
as soon as I returned home to the Countess. For five years
the manuscript remained obscure in a drawer, growing a
shroud of its own fine dust. It eventually made my name as
a singer, and the revenue from it has supported me ade-
quately for the last fifteen years.

They needed twenty men to remove all the bodies.

I left first, on a stretcher. Raoul insisted.

After a search that lasted two days and turned up nothing
(an anxious time for me) Raoul decided with the managers
to seal up the secret passage leading from the office to the
hidden stairs. They used a solid slab of marble this time, to
keep out the Ghost. In addition to this, every outdoor
entrance they found was filled with earth and cemented
over. The newspapers said that it was an appropriate tomb
for the Opera Monster. Who knows, if Erik did die (and I
have no way of knowing otherwise), I would say that was
right.

Philippe woke from his slumber in his own huge bed,
the day after his adventure in the basement. He had no
memory at all of the week proceeding, and he had to be
shown the letter that Madame Giry wrote to convince him
that any of it had happened at all. The soldiers recovered in
a charity hospital, and were totally paid off.

As for me, I lost everything. In order to avoid a scandal
I volunteered nothing of my motives, agreeing with everything that Raoul surmised. Not even my fiancée could keep
my name from the papers, but I was depicted as the delicate
victim, who stayed pure. My name was touted through soci-
ety. I found myself much in demand at the 'better' kinds of
parties, where the people of the theatre could never go.

Raoul and I were married three weeks later, in the church in Brittany. The priest performed the wedding without charging us. I wore a new snowy dress, a hand-made lace veil, and the roses in my bouquet were white. The Countess and Philippe were our only witnesses. We honeymooned for two weeks in Florence. I settled in to being a wife. It was a life without song.

15.

I sang *Don Juan Triumphant* again tonight, it was the tenth revival tour. The opera is a perennial hit, and I am always, always cast as Doña Ana. It has got to the point that I feel like I am playing a parody of myself as I once was; the passionate, dark-haired post-adolescent who wanted nothing out of life but the freedom to sing. Well, I finally have it. It comes at a cost.

I stood under the new, hot gaslights, greasepaint melting down my face, my greying scalp itching beneath the wig I wear, a mockery of my own former chestnut curls. I clasped my hands above my white dress, in agony at my loss of innocence, singing, 'For oftentimes it is when Pegasus seems winning the race, he sprains a wing and down we tend, like Lucifer hurled from heaven!'

Byron would laugh, if he were not so long buried. Erik and I inverted his romantic parody, applying his lines to our own script in a way that held the plot before a mirror so that comedy reversed itself to tragedy. Well, now it has become comedy again. The Don Juan that I sing to now on stage is fifteen years my junior. He woos me like a gentleman rogue; I simper like a girl.

Leaving the stage, I knew that Raoul was out there,

somewhere, in the audience. He comes to watch every one of my performances, though since the divorce was finalised in court (a scandal I weathered, though it nearly did unseat me from my chances at fame) he has respected my wishes, ceased sending his sad little flowers, and stopped attempting to contact me after the final curtain winds down.

It has been over a decade since the last time I found him, uninvited, in my rooms. I am certain that Madame Giry had much to do with that. After the suicide of Little Meg (who could not live without beauty), she was, in pity, promoted to House Inspector in charge of security. She is the first woman to ever hold that position and, at sixty-five years old, she remains effective in the role. There have been no more robberies in the foyer; she routed all the pickpockets. There have been fewer fights among the Lords. I needed her help. Even after the first round of paperwork went through the courts I am convinced that Raoul still believed that someone else, some unseen presence, was forcing me to leave him. He couldn't understand why on earth I would want to leave the life he built for me, safe in his shadow, where the only thing that worried my pretty little head was maintaining my body to build status for him.

Even after five years of marriage I doubt that he rightly heard a single word that came out of my mouth. Of course, by the time we were married, when I buried my hopes in favour of him, nearly every word I spoke was couched in lies. It took me half a decade to build up the nerve to start telling the truth.

By that time my luck had turned. His brother Philippe, poor man, never recovered from the death of La Sorelli. I remember going with Raoul to visit him, three years after my abduction. We found him lying in his enormous bed; it was absurd in the small rooms he took in the Hotel de Bouvier after ceding the mansion to my husband as a wedding gift. He called the bed 'the site of my greatest joy in life' and insisted that it make the move along with his other, more portable possessions. I believe that the workmen were forced to remove the two huge panes of the picture window that the room boasted – a feat they managed, somehow, without breaking either sheet of glass – in order to force its passage to the room.

Philippe was fading fast by then. I could see that he had lost quite a bit of weight; even smothered as he was in counterpanes his body seemed sunken. Well, I could relate to that. I was growing fairly thin myself. His skin and eyes were yellow (that gave me a start!) and the skin sagged beneath his shadowed sockets. Even when he slept his fingers never released from the stoppered neck of the bottle he clutched.

When he saw us he smiled, called Raoul and I over to sit beside him on the bed. He laid his claw-like hand on mine and, in a broken voice, he said, 'True love is a treasure that should never be squandered.' He pulled his brother's hand to mine so that all three of us were joined together, 'I am so glad that you have found completion in each other. You strengthen one another, and in your love, neither is reduced.'

He died three weeks later. In accordance with his will the massive bed was burnt. He was buried with a small sample of the ashes in one hand, contained inside of a locket shaped like a heart. In the other he held a small, worn, dancing slipper.

After the funeral, Raoul said, 'I cannot understand it. Why did he throw away his life like that? She was a fool and a whore; wholly unworthy of him.'

I did not reply; I had learned by then that it was better not to bother. Besides, I felt so cold inside that few things could fire me into any complex discourse. It was as though the shivering shock I'd felt underground had never really departed. Riding back from the funeral my teeth chattered in my skull.

It took me two more years to finally leave him. I admit, to Raoul it had probably seemed sudden. Really, I had decided before the funeral. My mind was made up in the moment that his brother joined our hands together and spoke those blasphemous words on the subject of love.

Raoul came home one night after a day-long absence. He called for me to join him in the library where he was sipping brandy and indulging in a cigar that stank like burning cat fur. He rose when I entered, offering me a seat by the fire. I gazed into the flames, lost in a robe that had fitted me a year ago, rubbing my arms to keep me free from the cold. Raoul offered me a blanket. As I was tucking it around my legs, he told me that after two years of struggle (the company hadn't played to a capacity audience since the night that I left) he had sold his shares in the Palais Garnier to a foreign investor who worked from afar. Raoul had never met the man, he did all of his work through an agent, but he seemed to know what he was doing and had already begun implementing plans designed to keep the theatre from shutting its doors. This man, a Monsieur Reynard, immediately fired the managers that I had known and hired two others more fitting for his purposes. Raoul had turned a tidy profit through these negotiations, and he was proud of it.

He could not understand why I continued to press him for the less-important details; which dancers remained, which members of the orchestra had been fired, who sang the lead roles? All of this was entirely unrelated to profit, and uncomfortably reminded him of our own unfortunate history.

Raoul looked at me, his bland face clouding with concern, saying, 'Christine, I knew that I shouldn't have told you all of this. The doctor was right when he forbade you to attend the performances. They were unsettling your womb.' He came around behind me, massaged my neck. It felt like a stranglehold. He continued, 'Perhaps that is why we have never had children. For the sake of your health, I will say no more.'

He kissed me, once, upon the forehead. 'Now be a good girl, and go off to bed.'

It was the last time that I ever obeyed him.

The next morning, after Raoul rolled over on to my side of the bed, I showed him my back. He shrugged, good-naturedly, kissed me, and went down to breakfast.

I remained between two sheets, staring at the celling until I heard the front door slam and the clatter of hooves against cobbles as the white carriage rolled him off to his day at the trade-offices. I saw, in my mind's eye, the horses as they strained against the traces, their hair streaming with sweat, running until the bonds that held them broke.

I got up once I was certain that he was gone for good. I rang the bell for the maid, a girl of seventeen who favoured overlarge garments. Her slatternly mob cap slid over one eye, lending her a strange, cycloptic look. She was shocked at my orders. It had been years since I asked her for breakfast.

Once I had eaten, pastry and ham, a third of a small, jam-spread baguette, I dressed in maroon silk (bemoaning the way my figure had withered – the fabric flapped around me) and began, quickly, to pack.

I took only what I thought that I would need to live, luxurious things that had a high retail value; the jewellery, of course, what loose gold came easily to hand, all of my most expensive dresses. I took my music box, as well. The cymbals that the stuffed monkey held jangled as I slid it into the bottom of the suitcase; this was one thing that I did not intend to rid myself of. Since, as my husband, he legally owned everything that I brought into the marriage (including my person) he could have called the constable to fetch me from my adoptive mother's house. He never did, supposing that this was but a temporary illness on my part. A fever better starved than fed with attention.

As for the Countess, when I arrived on her doorstep she was ecstatic, greeting me with open arms and practically pulling me across the threshold. She had, it seemed, never approved of our union though she had hesitated to say so at the time, fearing that her disapproval would be misinterpreted. And, in truth, it might have been, although not by myself.

Immediately, she began helping me to plan my escape, her blue eyes blazing in her glorious Nordic ruin of a face. She poured the strong tea she favoured into a cup of delicate red porcelain saying, 'Well, my dear, where to begin? You have no funds of your own, I expect. I shall hire the lawyer.' She laughed, 'After this is over I shall finally be able to write you back into my will.'

I flinched at that. She leaned forward, patted my knee, 'No offence my dear, but had I died he would have inherited, and I could not have borne knowing that one day, while my corpse was rotting, that idiot boy would be trampling my carpets and selling off my land.'

'Yes,' I said, 'he was counting on doing just that. The forest you own in Britany would have been sold to a shipyard.'

She laughed, 'Of course he was! Why do you think he would risk attempting to clip the wings of an artist, unless the risk would pay him.' She refilled my cup. 'Enough of that. In six months or so you will be a free woman.'

Her eyes glittered. 'I have very good lawyers. Now is the time to discuss your future. You are still young, my pet, the whole world before you. What is it you want?'

I had to laugh with her. It had been so long since anyone had asked me that. I took her warm hand, said, 'I want to sing.'

She squeezed back, 'Then you shall. The Opera House has new managers, of a progressive political bent. Once you are free you will have two points of leverage; your marvellous voice – no one could take that from you – and the score you brought back from the pit.' She paused, 'Unless you left it at that idiot's house. If you have, I could get it. Claim that you did not own it when you brought it. We'll have to have it if it is as good as you said it was, it will help with contract negotiations. I'll find proof somewhere of a previous claim....'

I interrupted her, 'No, no Maman,' it was her turn to startle, I'd never called her by that name before. She had been afraid to ask me. 'The score is in this very house. In the desk, in my bedroom.'

She smiled with relief, 'So that is that.'

And so it was. While the papers were filed and my status shifted from married to separated and on to divorced, I practised every day, returning my voice almost to the height of its lustre, though there was a new veil across my lower register that added a sense of sorrow to whatever I sang as a mezzo. I had finally learned to sing for myself, wearing the roles I chose and no other. It was difficult, satisfying work, returning to myself. I was happier than I had been in years and, for a while, I stopped dreaming of the face I saw, once, deep below the surface of the earth.

In the end my guardian was right about everything. The new managers had heard about the quality of my voice, and they were indeed progressive – if that term means that they were willing to see profit in scandal. They paid me more than double my usual salary, triple if you include the fee I negotiated for the rights to my opera. And as for the scandal, the newspaper headlines shouting, 'Divorced Diva Dares the Stage!' filled them with pride. The right kind of scandal can stuff a lot of gold into coffers. My divorce was considered exceptionally daring; they milked it for all that it was worth.

I played the role of Carmen exclusively for a full five years, to a packed house. There is nothing quite so exciting to a certain type of audience as a fallen woman, dressed in crimson, displaying her beautiful sorrow before all the world.

By the time I finally got to debut *Don Juan Triumphant* I was thoroughly sick of playing the Gypsy. My opera was greeted with lukewarm reviews; I was even then a little too old to be playing a fresh-faced maiden like Ana, and besides, I couldn't give credit where it was properly due. The critics believed that it had been written by a woman and they judged it accordingly.

In spite of that, possibly because of that, the crowds clamoured for it. I performed two encores at every showing. The seats were always sold. The intake was enormous. It still packs the house in its once-yearly revival show. Whoever the invisible theatre-owner was, he must have been pleased by the revenue. I never met him. He never wrote me any notes or contacted me in any way, save through his managers. I assumed that he enjoyed the hypocrisy of gaining profit from a source whose morality he disapproved of. In nearly fifteen years he never so much as sent flowers to my room.

But Monsieur Reynard is gone now, whoever he was. He has sold his stock to the company of Andre and Reichmann. And I am growing tired of singing the same damned roles. I do not know how long I will continue to endure it.

Sitting before my mirror now, my ageing face garbed round with plaster angels whose beauty never fades, or changes, I strip off the wig I wore on stage and let down my own sweat-dampened tresses. I am ready for a change that goes beyond a coat of grease-paint and a flattering wardrobe. The paint is terrible for the skin, in any case. A mask is no good if it cakes in my wrinkles.

In a moment I will have to dress again, don my fancy party clothes to flirt and preen with my new managers, earning my keep. I dab my neck with more of Monsieur Andre's wonderful, outrageous perfume and, God knows why, I start singing an excerpt from the redemption scene that takes place when Don Juan and Doña Ana are reunited in heaven at the very end of the play.

It is a musically complicated verse, 'Between two worlds life hovers like a star, 'twixt night and the morn, upon the horizon's verge.' Somewhere, somehow, the music has swung again, away from comedy. But it isn't a tragedy any more, not the way I'm singing it now. If I didn't know any better, listening to myself, I would have to say that my spirit was rejoicing.

I finish, hitting all of the high tones, 'How little do we know that which we are!'

As the last note dies, I hear a knock at my door. I shout, 'Come!'

It isn't the girl I expected, the little foul-toothed rat who has been serving as my dresser, coming to say that the managers are ready for me to charm investors in the foyer. It's Madame Giry, dressed in her usual ratty black crepe, leaning on the man's walking stick she uses to keep the box-boys in line. There is a letter in her hand, a thick envelope, written on expensive linen paper. She smiles at me inscrutably as I take it.

My name, my old name, is written across the front in handwriting I know.

ERIK

13.

I climbed from the bed where I'd buried Christine to save her from the fumes of the Lethe and the fire from the guns. Her would-be lover had forced himself through the fog; either passion or an incredible lung capacity had rescued him from the same sleep his minions had succumbed to. I did not notice him at first. I had no time to count the numbers of the rescue party. There were nine men on the floor.

I gave the big blond a kick to test the effectiveness of my drug; the black toe of my brogue landed between his armpit and his hip. He flinched reflexively. Good, I thought. He will recover in every capacity. Christine will be pleased.

I called to her, 'Christine! All is well. You can come out now!'

And that was when the boy attacked me. He had stalked me from the shadows, hiding behind a pillar or perhaps the large wardrobe. He shouted, 'Monster!' and fired his gun at the same instant that I turned to face him. If his hand had not been shaking there is no doubt that I would have been dead; he was standing less than three feet behind me. Luckily, the bullet flew into the door of the cabinet, piercing a dress.

I leaped forward, striking at the gun with my foot. The

sharp heel of my shoe collided with his wrist and I had the satisfaction of seeing the gun clatter to the floor. I had disarmed him, but it wasn't enough. I was, I am, more than fifteen years older than he is. The difference in prowess between a boy of twenty and a man at the edge of his prime is surprisingly vast. I was quick on my feet; I'd had some experience fighting. He was faster, and poisoned by wrath. It acted on his blood like a compound of coca leaf.

The boy leaped at me, pinning me face down on the tiles at the edge of the pool. His knees were digging into my kidneys. He was binding my wrists with a length of rough rope that he must have had on his person. I scanned the room, seeking another gun, a knife, anything I could use as a weapon. I could see a revolver still clutched in the hand of the nearest attacker; he looked like an out-of-luck soldier that the boy had hired for the evening like a suit. There was no hope of reaching it, my bonds were too tight; the reach was too far.

I couldn't think. My head was swimming with anxiety. I hadn't been this close to another man since I left Monsieur Garnier. I was frightened, also, for Christine.

I saw her head, her dear dark eyes, appear over the lip of the pool that I had furnished for her bed. She looked terrified. My lungs were compressed, but I had enough power to throw my voice in her direction. I gave her a message, 'No Christine, no. Remain perfectly still. Do nothing. I love you too well to see your life ruined.' Brave girl, she obeyed, sinking back beneath the blankets, but Raoul must have seen her because he dragged me to my feet and hauled me towards the nearest pillar, stretching upwards until he hung me like a scarecrow from the brass light fixture. My shoulders screamed in protest at this treatment; my head swam with blinding pain. He struck me in the stomach several times for good measure, so hard that my diaphragm spasmed. I could not speak. The metal was so hot that it burnt my wrists.

Leaving me there, he ran back to the pool and fetched out my darling. She was pale, shivering, unable to stand. To his credit, he handled her delicately – as though she were composed of china. He settled her into a chair, tucking a blanket around her limbs. When he loosened the scarf that served as an air-filter her poor teeth started chattering. It was probably shock.

The boy was not finished. Part of me rather hoped that he would take her and leave, returning later with help to rescue his friends. If he had done so, I am certain that I would have been able to work the ropes against the bar until they frayed and I freed myself. I would run, as fast as I could, to one of my more hidden bunkers, well stocked with food, medicine, and mental stimulation. After a few weeks, when the furore had died down, I would emerge again and rescue Christine.

It wasn't to be. The little Comte wasn't finished. He left her sitting in the chair, facing me. Our eyes met. Hers were wide, too wide, and filled with terror. I would have given anything to calm her. I could only stare.

The boy was limping a little now. Good, I exhausted him. I would have been disgusted with myself if I had not managed at least that. He bent beside the man that I had kicked – I recognised him now as his own elder brother, the one in love with the dancer, La Sorelli; now deceased. Raoul pried the gun from his hand and slouched back to me.

Christine, thank God, could not see the way that the maniac was grinning; his smile split from ear to ear as though he were telling himself a good dirty joke. He stood beside me, breathing almost into my ear, raising the gun until the black barrel penetrated the eye socket of my mask nearly touching my eyeball.

For the first time in nearly twenty years, since my time in the nunnery, I said a prayer to Our Lord.

He withdrew the barrel. I thought it was mercy.

Then he turned to Christine and said, 'Do you not wish to look upon the face of your abductor?'

I knew I was damned.

He tore off my mask, my wig in one smooth motion, revealing my face which is so much like the skull of a corpse.

Christine saw me. Her face contorted with fear and repugnance; she vomited onto the floor.

By the time that he shot me I knew which was mercy; I would rather have died then, than live with the memory of her disgust. Unconsciousness claimed me.

I spent a long time in a darkness that I mistook for hell. I saw hideous visions. My mother, screaming at me when I tried to kiss her; the face of the old nun who told me terror tales night after night in the dark; the villagers who toured the carnival that purchased me, their twisted faces leering as they threw their rotten fruit. If Hell is any worse than that, we are right to fear it.

When I awoke I found that I was alone in utter darkness, buried beneath soft layers of carpet, blankets, a few scattered stuffed animals. I panicked, until the sharp stab of pain in my side recalled the past to me and provided my mind with a modicum of focus.

I have no idea how long I slept, and I have no way of finding out. By the time I hauled myself, with much agony, from the bed that I had been placed in I had enough energy to light a nearly full-length taper from a candelabrum that I groped from her dresser, before collapsing to the floor again, blacking out.

By the time I resurfaced, the candle had burnt down to a stub a half-inch in length and the brass stand had been glued to the floor in a puddle of wax. The first thing I saw was the crushed remnant of my mask, smashed into splinters at the foot of a pillar that had been bathed in my blood.

I gave myself a thorough examination and found that I had two small holes above my left hip; an entrance and an exit. They had been washed and bound with Christine's white scarf, now crusted, stinking with blood and infection. I smiled, my mouth flooding with bitterness. It was she who saved me, then, despite her disgust.

The candle was guttering. I reached into the pocket of my coat, seeking another Lucifer, and instead my hand withdrew with a folded sheet of stationery. I gave up my search for the matches, using the rest of the light to locate another candlestick that I ignited from the source just before the last of the flame turned blue and guttered out.

I opened the note. It was her handwriting. Ten words:

Erik, I love you. Forgive me. I'll lie to him.

She left me. She wrote that after she had seen my face. It almost made the trouble worth it. I could live the rest of my life on the memory.

I blacked out again after reading it, rising several hours later, the note in my hand, the candle extinguished.

It took me the better part of the day to return to my chambers, hauling my carcass across the floor in the darkness. By the time I made it I was delirious with infection and dehydration. My arms felt as though they had been half-wrenched from their sockets. Thankfully, I had set aside supply of laudanum, alcohol, and a powder made of white willow bark to quell the infection. I had a good supply of preserved food in my cache. Even if I had not been severely injured I would have needed those stores to save me – three months into my recovery I discovered that the managers had treated their Opera Ghost problem with the same level of ingenuity that the rest of Paris applied to disposing of rats; they had sealed me in, blocked every entrance and exit I'd made with hardened cement.

For nine months I battled against a dangerous blood infection. I spent the following four months burrowing out of the basement like an escaping prisoner. Towards the end of my time, before I escaped into moonlight, I was reduced to catching sewer rats in traps and roasting them on fires that I built by burning first the doors, and then the furniture. Luckily, I had a good supply of chairs left over from the construction of the theatre – my original plans had called for nearly double the seats as were finally installed. None of this saved me from madness. Every night I dreamed again of the cage, my humiliation, my filth, their flung garbage.

Occasionally I saw her face in sleep again and, in spite of her note, I relived her disgust.

Over a year passed before I saw the moon again. I had a well; I had water, so I washed my body and my clothes. I dressed in suit, in hat, in cloak, and emerged through a crack in the wall like a ghost. I spent all of that first night out-of-doors, walking the park, touching the bark of the trees with my bare fingers. It was beautiful; a sensation I'd forgotten. Living wood is so much different in feel from furniture.

I sat beneath a laurel tree and thought. By the time that I had reached my conclusions the dew had fallen. My bare face was wet with it. I had barely enough time before rosy-fingered dawn drew back her curtain to purchase supplies at the river market. My bare face allowed me to make my selections without harassment – and in some cases, without making payment. I found that there were hidden benefits to the honesty of terror. I wondered why I had not tried this before.

On my return to my home I saw that the opera house was still under reconstruction. I would have time to rebuild my passages, not that I expected that I would need to use them – Christine would be married by now, forbidden from singing – but they were familiar to me, it would be comforting to have the option of the occasional free show. Who knows, I thought, she might sell the rights to *Don Juan*. I could see a production.

Time passed. I set down to work. I played music. I tried to forget her. Eventually, when records became available in the riverside market (about six months after they turned up in the homes of the wealthy), I purchased a gramophone. I never did use those corridors I'd spent three years rebuilding.

And then, one night, I read in the paper that the Palais Garnier was failing; Comte Phillipe was dead, Andre and Firmin were on the edge of bankruptcy. I could not allow it to close; it seemed like every hope I'd ever treasured had been buried in its walls. I could not let it fall into ruin again. Luckily, I retained a few old contacts from my days as an architect; though, it is true, they did not know me by face or even my true name. I wrote a letter which I posted at midnight, using the new boxes the government had conveniently installed almost under every lamp post.

Eventually, a response came. I read it, and felt myself return to life.

14.

When periods of happiness are described in books they are almost always insufferably boring. Nothing exciting seems to happen, and when it does it is entirely internal, growing like a disease beneath the skin of the world. This is why fairy tales are so fond of that classical summary, 'and they lived happily ever after'. If we heard the day-to-day minutiae of the Prince and Princess's marital bliss we would be tempted to murder. On the other end of the scale, I am sorry to report that protracted misery comes across to the reader in much the same fashion. Nothing seems to happen, nothing seems to change. Every day becomes the same miserable slog, the same stasis. And it is true, nothing does change; externally.

I endured this limbo for twenty miserable years following the abduction of Christine; two decades of nothing to report but an encroaching bitterness that, before I knew her, I would have leavened with a little healthy malice. But the years the Opera House stood empty robbed me of my appetite for ghost-work. I committed no murders.

I wasted time, or spent it. I tried to work; designing buildings, composing music, without success, rarely getting beyond the first basic notes. I produced the occasional sculpture in soapstone, a technique I learned in childhood. They generally began well enough, but I was inevitably forced to abandon them when I realised that I was releasing nothing but the same repeated face. The same wide eyes, the same look of disgust.

By the time that I read about the possible closure of the theatre I was close to suicidal. That morning I had woken late, and spent several hours beneath my red sheets, staring up at the celling. I remembered that it was possible to overdose on my sleeping serum and I wondered why I had not thought of anything so brilliantly easy before. I pondered; why did I survive my time in the carnival, my own blighted childhood, if only for this?

And then, that very morning, I happened across the notice of sale and wrote the letter that I mentioned before. Assuming the name of Monsieur Reynard – an improbable name for the Englishman I played, I realise, but gold precludes all questions – and contacted an agent I knew of that my Master Garnier had used to arrange the construction of his Paris home while he and I were working for the Persian Shah.

I listed the acceptable non-negotiable terms of purchase (they were generous indeed, and as I was a practised hand at blackmail, I could afford to be generous) and told my agent that he was only to contact me in order to confirm a sale; at which time he would hire the two gentlemen I'd named to serve as managers. Once this was done, they were to do everything possible to keep the doors open, even resorting to acceptable levels of scandal. Nothing on earth packs a theatre like the rumours of an affair, a bastard, or a murder. Even decent people feed on a whiff of the devil.

The managers could contact me only though a mail drop I had selected, and they should do so only in the event of a catastrophe on the scale of a fire (which I would be well-enough aware of anyway) or a financial crisis devastating enough to threaten the opera as an entity performed behind these walls.

The young Comte agreed to everything at once, as I knew that he would. He was as deeply in love with money as he imagined he was with my darling Christine. Raoul had reason to despise my Opera House, God knows he rarely passed its gilded threshold or bothered with the office work. As for Christine, her worst prophecies had come true. He never allowed her to visit at all, not even to sit under chaperone in their private opera box. If he had, then, before our sundering scabbed in my heart, I would have been unable to restrain myself from visiting her.

As for the managers I'd hired, they were very skilled. By simple application of common-sense business methods they boosted seat-sales enough to begin turning a modest profit, though my encouragement of scandal had to wait a while, until the right players presented themselves.

First, they hired a beautiful unmarried mezzo; a voluptuous blonde originally from Germany, to sing the witchy roles. Her voice was middling, but she was a lovely creature, and she came with a small child whose last-name was not her own. I followed the newspaper coverage with interest, and watched as the balance in Monsieur Reynard's bank-account flourished and grew.

A few months later Christine appeared at their door, newly divorced and demanding a contract. They had heard of her from their predecessors and were more than willing to negotiate on the strength of her early reviews. I read about her return in the paper; a tawdry portrait of a brazen, immoral female-composer who shone briefly in her youth (they wrote about her youth as though it were behind her. She was only 25!) who came trampling down the doorways and demanding to be treated as a diva.

The crucifix-clutching reporters lamented the declining

morality of the City of Lights; imagine a strumpet performing on stage! They admonished the last bastions of
morality to shun the Palais Garnier and never darken those
faux-gilt doors with their Christian coinage.

Who knows, perhaps the population of people with an
interest in the heaven that comes after earth did stay away.
They were not missed. The rest of the city came out in
droves to see an angel sing on earth. For the first five years
of her return we had a packed house every night, though I
suspect that, given Christine's curiosity and driving need
for challenging roles, she grew rather tired of portraying
Carmen.

I admit that I was tempted, sorely tempted, to contact
her after I read the announcement of her second debut. I
remember that I sat at my desk, grappling with myself, gripping the sides of the writing surface so hard that the wood
splintered and I peeled the skin from my fingers like a shell
from an egg. But in the end I managed to chill my desires
and refrain from my pen.

I did it by remembering the look on her face the last
time I saw her, her repulsion so deep that it brought up her
vomit. Ten words written in comforting haste could not
erase the wound she inflicted in her surprised innocence.
And then I remembered what brought her to me in the
first place. It was my goal to help her to rise high enough
in the service of art to be worthy of our composition, our
Don Juan, and to help her earn the clout to bring it into
production.

As for Christine, I had been primarily her teacher, a
means to an end. She wanted a life on the stage more
than anything, and I had helped her to get it. Her feelings
for me, whatever they were, were the passion of a girl

held in close proximity with one man only – for want of a choice she had chosen the monster. Until she saw his face. The brief time we had was rather like a candle; easily extinguished, in spite of the foolish kiss I gave her cheek. It was time for me to let her go.

After five years playing Carmen she had her chance to bring Don Juan to prominence, and of course she took it. She sang the role of Ana with such poignancy that hearing the faint strains of her aria, even through metres of bedrock and thick-tiled floor, was too much for me. I took to visiting the markets a little earlier than usual, to escape the sound of her living voice. I never saw the production live, you see, I had no wish to risk weakening my resolve.

When I re-entered the world I discovered a surprise. Ten years ago I would have expected to be arrested immediately for the crime of extreme ugliness. I believed, to my bones, that the world was merely biding its time to stick me in a cage again, or in the ground. But, as it turned out, a hooded cape was enough – it washed me in shadow, and even the constabulary ignored this ghost.

Our opera outlasted the original release, spanning a full year and spawning recordings, reprintings, and a yearly revival. And while the critics damned it with the faintest praise that they could muster; written, as it seemed, by a young girl, the public adored it. And when I eventually pur-chased a recording (her voice was safe enough to manage, flattened onto a grooved disk) it was as wonderful as I knew it would be. I wept freely for the first time in my life.

Oh it was bitter to have authored a structure even more wonderful than the Opera House and then have to endure knowing that the credit would forever be ascribed to another. My only consolation lay in the fact that the 'other' was her. We were connected, eternally, in art even if no one else knew it. It did not even matter, really, if Christine allowed herself to acknowledge it in the solitude of her thoughts.

Years passed, as they will, and even to me they seemed changeless. Perhaps the years themselves were changeless. After all, spring bled into summer, summer died into autumn and the bones of the winter rose through the skin of autumn's rot. So, just possibly, the world was in stasis.

I was not.

I found myself submitting my ego to tests. I went outside, earlier, and more frequently, constantly maskless. The idea of hiding had become suddenly repulsive. Sometimes I even emerged into twilight. I never did risk the sun. It had been too long since we had greeted each other.

My face was as abhorrent as usual, but after Christine's dramatic reaction the disgust of mere mortals no longer frightened me. Besides, my body had changed – not in structure, I was still hardly more than a skeleton, however strong – but I held myself more firmly erect and, in the river market at least, monstrosity was respected. This was especially true when it came with a reputation for a willingness to fight. I did not, at that time, understand the cause of my sudden acceptance of the truth of my nature, but I realise now that it was a symptom of the spiritual callouses I'd formed. In short, I still wore my cloak, my wide hat, as a courtesy to the unsuspecting, I have always loathed to make a child cry, but I no longer cared that those who did manage to peer beneath my hood were terrified.

My context had changed; I was finally free of the mental cage I'd been walking around in, carrying with me. Perhaps it came from growing older. I was (it shocked me) nearly fifty-five years old; beyond the expected mid-point of my life.

The sweet taste of freedom added to the cup that otherwise brimmed with bitterness was enough to make it palatable. For the first time in over twenty years I was happy to live.

I came to enjoy walking in the parks. I found myself enthralled by the sight of the green haze of twilight darkening like a bruise until the sky joined with the crowned heads of the trees and bled into blackness. The night, in late spring, was unspeakably beautiful. I had taken a seat on a wrought-iron bench lodged in the shadow of an enormous, leaf-rich oak. I was watching the flitting forms of bats flicker against the gas-light, engaged in their own small glories; their battles, their courtships, defeats, carving the warm air with their wings and shrieking with ecstasy.

And that was when I saw Christine, walking alone on the little path, dressed in an expensive rose-coloured walking costume and leaning a little on her pink parasol as though she had injured a knee.

She was much changed, so much so that at first I did not recognise her, mistaking her for an ordinary, attractive, middle-aged woman; only something in her posture, in the delicate arc of her neck caught my heart like a fishhook. When she turned her head to scan the shadows (a move made, I am certain, entirely by instinct) I saw her eyes and lost all doubt that it was Christine's spirit lodged in that too-thin body, her voice behind that fading skin.

All of these years, when I thought of her, I had been picturing the wild, laughing girl I knew; not this sad-eyed woman.

Christine walked off, vanishing into the darkness without

glancing back. Had she been Orpheus, Eurydice would have been dragged out of hell, ready to live. I braced my hands on my knees, held my head down between them. My mouth filled with the fear-taste of copper carried on a flood of saliva. It was a long while before I could comfortably breathe, or trust that my intestines remained where God placed them.

In all fairness, this delusion of her eternal youth was not entirely the product of a romantic illusion. She was still frequently reviewed and the critics never described her as anything but vibrantly young and exceptionally beautiful. And, in truth, once my body overcame its shock I understood that although she was a girl no longer, she had only just entered the middle-age. In short, although she was a ghost of the girl I knew, she remained entirely herself, and seen that way, she remained glorious. Whoever she was now, however she thought of herself, whatever changes had occurred, whatever small deaths, she remained my genius; I wanted to know her again.

As soon as I could walk, I returned to my home, to the desk that we had once covered with poetry to be converted to song. I sat down and wrote:

Dear Miss Daaé (or may I be so bold as to address you as 'Christine?'),

You saved my life once, long ago, and I have been inexcusably remiss in thanking you for providing that service.

I do not know how the world has treated you; externally, at least, your life appears to be progressing quite well. You sing beautifully still, although your voice has grown a bit veiled regarding your lower register, and while the opera that we wrote together has received mixed reviews, you have not. You have, rightfully, been greeted with enthusiasm every time that you have appeared on stage.

Of course you knew me quite well, once. You anticipate the 'but'. Here it is, the fly in your soup: It has come to my attention that you are not entirely happy, that you may, in fact, be miserable in your lot. I imagine that it is difficult for an artist of your calibre to content herself to the same tired roles. I would like to propose a solution.

I know that you are meant to join the new managers in the foyer for tonight's fundraising gala. I know this because they, like their predecessors, are in my employ. If, instead, you would be so kind as to meet me in our former haunt (the flies where we reached the closest to heaven that I, at least, shall ever come) I would like to propose a renewal of our partnership in the pursuit of an operatic work whose beauty has never before been seen on this earth.

Should you find this proposal agreeable, there are two things that you should know. The first is that I will not wear a mask again. I am aware that the last time we met, as it were, face-to-face I quite badly disturbed you. Lately I have disposed of artifice (as applied to myself). If this appalls you, do not approach. I will feel no offence.

The second stipulation is this: If you choose to join me, come to me as you are now. Do not attempt to be what you were. The past is a foreign country to us, and we cannot ever apply for re-entry. The future is also very strange, but we cannot avoid that border. Whether we cross it together or not is entirely up to you.

Do not bother with a response. Come to me, or do not. That will be answer enough.

Thank you, my dear, for saving my life.

I remain yours,
Erik

When I was satisfied, both with what I had written and with what I had omitted to write, I tipped Madame Giry five francs to deliver the envelope to her rooms after the last curtain.

The flies were very dirty; no one had bothered with them in a long time. There were new conventions, now, for changing the scenery. No one had ever retaken the role of flies-Master. No spirit but mine occupied the rafters.

While I waited I kicked a few desiccated pigeons on to the floor, they fell slowly, like clumps of dead leaves. Otherwise I left everything as it was when I arrived. I laid no carpets this time, lit no candles. Everything must be exactly as it seemed if we were to meet again.

15.

I did not expect her to come. In composing my letter, I considered refraining from telling her about my abandonment of my disguise, but in the end I decided against it. I knew that she would have been more likely to dare the approach if she thought that my monstrosity were covered, but that omission, that lie, would have been a bad basis for building a beginning on. Worse, possibly, than not beginning at all.

Besides, I told myself, she was a girl then, with little experience in the world. Perhaps, after all of this time, we could meet on level ground.

Somehow I doubted it. I remembered, too clearly, the last look that she had given me. I remembered the vomit, fresh on her lips.

The party began in the foyer. I heard music, the piano, the strings, and a woman's high laughter. Soon the great staircase I built would be swarming with waiters bearing bottles, glasses that brimmed with champagne, trays laden with hors d'oevres and canapés. Soon there would be dancing: women swaying in bright-coloured taffeta brushing against the bodies of the creatures who loved them.

Well, I was also dressed for a party. My wide brimmed hat, my dinner jacket, my silk cravat were impeccable and, I noticed, glancing into the mirror, slightly obscene beneath the gross face of a corpse. I never had to try very hard to achieve a dramatic effect.

I turned away from the ladder leading up to my platform. I leaned over the railing and remembered my disposal of Jacques, contemplating the drop, the sound of meat-splatter. It was so easy to fall.

And that was when I heard it, the soft sound of a silk shoe gaining traction on iron. She was coming after all; she risked mounting the ladder.

I did not turn, but I straightened my back, so that I would be standing at my full height when we met. Her breathing was as musical as it ever was. I wanted to hear her behind me; I wanted to know that she was there, not three feet from my skin. I wanted this so that, even when she ran, I would have something to treasure forever, the knowledge that she had returned to see me at last.

I heard the sound of her mounting the final step, felt the scaffold vibrate as she edged forward a few feet and then, suddenly, stopped. I heard her breath come faster. I did not know if it was fear or excitement, until she spoke.

'Erik?' He voice was trembling. So it was fright.

I would not turn and startle her. I would answer. We could, at least, speak.

'Christine.'

The blood was pounding in my skull. I hardly heard the sound of her sprinting. I felt the scaffold swinging as she ran. I felt the collision. It was almost an attack.

She wrapped her arms around my waist and buried her face into the back of my jacket, reaching around my chest and gripping my hands so fiercely that I felt my knuckles crack.

She was trembling, almost shuddering, and when her voice came again it was muffled by mucous and fabric, her throat, her great instrument, was terribly choked. 'You're alive, you're alive. I waited so long for you. I didn't know I was waiting. Thank God, you're alive.' She tried to turn me to face her, I stood firm.

She laughed, nervously, attempted to detangle herself from my clothes. Her will was as strong as her embarrassment, yet she could not manage it. She remained where she was, 'You said "Come as you are". Well, this is what I am, now. A silly old idiot. You haven't seen me yet.' Her voice suddenly chilled, softened, 'I am much changed, even from the shadow that I show on the stage. I feel like I have been trying, and failing, to remain who I was.'

She squeezed my hand, more gently this time. I ceased to worry about the buttons on my jacket.

'Oh Erik, please speak to me.'

I opened my mouth and found my voice had fled. I coughed, once, to clear it. 'I have seen you, my dear. Last night in the park. You walked beneath the streetlights. You looked almost as though you were weeping.'

And now it was my turn for trembling.

I let my free hand fall upon the scaffold, supporting myself, braced against metal. I said, 'You have changed, Christine, not beyond recognition, and the change is not unpleasing, but you are not the girl you were. You have altered. I, unfortunately, have not – or not enough.'

'You have not turned to face me.' She was not clinging now, merely resting her face between my shoulders. I could feel her warm breath through my silk. 'You came without your mask to test me. Do it.'

I drew a long breath, felt her detach herself from me, stepping backward into the dust.

I turned, happy to finally be able to look at her, terrified that it would not last, terrified of what I would see in the seconds before she fled.

It appeared that she shared my trepidation. Her hands were clenched at her sides, nails boring into her flesh. She was staring at my feet. I was pleased to see her face again, even bowed away from me. She was as beautiful as ever in the afternoon of life.

With a shock, I recalled that I was entering the evening myself. How had we survived so long without each other's voices?

Her dark eyes climbed my legs, lingered a moment on the place where the wound she bound formed a secret scar beneath my clothes. She shook herself, forced her head higher. When she looked up into my face her teeth were clenched, her muscles bunched beneath the skin. Her near-black eyes were focused as a hawk's.

I saw her body jerk with supressed repugnance, I saw her thighs tremble beneath her skirt, but she would not look away. She did not run. She took in every inch of my face, until our eyes locked, held. Finally, after what felt like a century had passed with me in the burning, her jaws relaxed. She smiled.

The expression was small, a little sickly round the edges, but it was real enough.

After a while, she spoke, 'Forgive me, please, for my revulsion. I cannot help it, but I will overcome myself.' She tried to take a step forward, and found that she could not manage it. 'I kissed you once, you know, while you were hanging there unconscious, before I brought your body down and hid it in the bed. I had to close my eyes to do it, but I did. Your breath was sweet. I have never forgotten.'

I smiled at her; she flinched slightly at the effect. I was sorry for that – it was the best that I could manage with the ruin I was born with – before her revelation rocked me like a hammer-blow and I felt myself sinking to the floor, spreading my legs across the filth, the dust and rat bones.

I could not control my voice when I spoke, and that frightened me. It was the one thing left to me that I could rely on, and now even that had fled. 'I had no idea.' I buried my face in my hands, a mercy for both of us. There was so much wasted time that we could have spent together, so many wasted years alone.

After a moment I heard the rustling of silk, felt the warmth of her body pressed so close to mine that if this were a play, we would have been considered obscene, an implied event occurring off-stage, to be hinted at only.

She leaned her head across my shoulder, spreading her faded hair across my collar. She spoke, 'And now I find that no matter the age we are always children sprawled in the dirt.' She laid her hand atop my own, covering the poison of my life with her soft flesh. 'We are filthy, stupid, but alive. Now that I know that you live, I will never leave your side.'

I had to laugh at that; I meant to laugh. It sounded like screaming, 'And how are we to manage, then, if I will not mask myself and you cannot stand to look at me?'

Self-blinded as I was, I felt her body shift until I could

not feel her. Convinced she was leaving, that I was missing my last glimpse of her, I reached out, groping for her hands in my fevered desperation.

I caught hold of her shoulders. They were inches from my chest. I had kept my eyes closed; now I opened them and found my Christine.

She was kneeling in front of me, her knees pressing into the waffled iron on either side of my thighs. Her face and dress were streaked with dirt, with clean paths her tears had carved for her.

Christine was looking at me; not staring. To her I was not some animal that needed to be caged. It was a soft look, kind, if a little ill around the edges. She reached forward, cupped my face in her hands, and in a firm voice that brooked no argument, she said 'Teach me again, Erik. You taught me to sing, now teach me to look. I am a fast student. I am ready to work.'

What could I say, but 'Yes'?

Acknowledgements

I would like to thank the following people for their encouragement and aid: Sarah Kennedy and Menna Elfyn, for setting me on the path; Tiffany Atkinson, for teaching me how to write a novel and being a brilliant poetical badass; the academic staff in the Creative Writing departments at Mary Baldwin College, the University of Wales Trinity Saint David, and Aberystwyth University; my poetry publishers, Cultured Llama, Oneiros Books, Lapwing, Indigo Dreams, and Three Drops Press; Penny Thomas, for taking a chance on my work and then editing it to a fine sheen; my very patient friends (you know who you are) for putting up with the angst which I would like to believe was artistic and charming but which was probably actually very annoying; and finally, last but not least, Matthew David Clarke for his unwavering love and support. I would also like to thank you, reader, for taking the time to travel with me this far down the road.

About the Author

Bethany W. Pope is an award-winning author. She has published several collections of poetry: *A Radiance* (Cultured Llama, 2012), *Crown of Thorns* (Oneiros Books, 2013), *The Gospel of Flies* (Writing Knights Press, 2014), *Undisturbed Circles* (Lapwing, 2014), and *The Rag and Boneyard* (Indigo Dreams, 2016). Her chapbook *Among The White Roots* will be released by Three Drops Press next autumn. *Masque* is her first novel.

Originally from America, Bethany has lived in five states and five countries including, for several years, an orphanage in South Carolina. She has now made the UK her permanent home. In her life, she has played many roles: minister's daughter; the monster under the stairs; farmhand; midwife for cattle; caster of lead printing plates; veterinarian's surgical assistant; high-school drop-out; roller-skate-wearing waitress; university lecturer – all of these things have contributed to her career as a writer. She knows a thing or two about wearing a mask.

Bethany is an avid sabre fencer. She lives with her husband and a small yellow budgie who answers to Diogenes. You can find out more about her work at BethanyWPope.com